PERFECT

BOOK 2 OF THE *JOHNSON FAMILY* SERIES

DELANEY DIAMOND

"Love is when the other person's happiness is more important than your own."

—H. Jackson Brown

CHAPTER ONE

Three years ago…

A million dollars. That's how much money he'd spent.

Daniella Barrett-Johnson stared at her husband in disbelief.

Cyrus Johnson sat in the cushioned chair in the sitting area of their master suite, legs spread wide, the top buttons of his shirt opened and the tie of his tux hanging loose around his neck. She'd held her questioning until after the dinner party, but the entire night she'd been wound as tight as rope, itching to ask him about what she'd been told.

She'd hoped he would tell her it wasn't true. That her ex-boyfriend, Roland DuBois, had lied when he'd said Cyrus had bought his debts for a million dollars in exchange for him breaking up with her and disappearing from her life. Not only had Cyrus not denied the story, he didn't see anything wrong with the bribe. He couldn't understand why she was upset. Had Roland not felt guilty and come clean to her, she would have never known.

Roland had come clean to her. Not Cyrus.

She'd seen his ruthless side before, but she hadn't considered she might become a victim of his tactics. Outside of being the CEO of Johnson Enterprises, his family's beer and restaurant empire, he had his own private investments. As recently as two weeks ago he'd outbid other investors to purchase a family-owned company. Within days he'd slashed half the workforce and installed his own people in upper and middle management. When she'd asked him how he could be so callous, he'd simply replied, *"I don't buy these companies to make friends. I buy them to make money."*

What a fool she had been to fall in love with him in the first place. She had seen some good in him once. But the more she got to know him, what good she had seen had been overshadowed by a string of behavior that demonstrated a glaring lack of conscience. Since he'd deceived her on this point, what other areas of their lives had he deceived her in? This was the last straw. He was not the man for her.

She couldn't spend the rest of her life with someone she couldn't trust, teetering back and forth between being proud to be on his arm one minute and ashamed of his behavior the next.

"I wanted you to tell me you didn't do this," she said. *Show some remorse.*

"Then I'd be a liar. I've never lied to you, and I never will."

"No, you'll just deceive me," she said.

"It was a means to an end." He spoke calmly, as if such behavior was an everyday occurrence. For him it probably was.

"Was it worth it? Did you get your money's worth?"

"I would have paid much more. Ten times as much to get rid of him so I could have you." His words should have made her feel better, but they didn't.

"Why did you have to have me? Why did you feel the need to pay someone to get them out of the way?" She waited, her stomach unsettled by the gnaw of apprehension.

"Because you have all the qualities I looked for in a wife, Dani," he replied. "That's why I chose you."

His answer should have been a compliment, but it disappointed her. If he'd given another reason, she might have considered forgiving him for the breach of trust.

"I'm the perfect woman," she said bitterly and without conceit.

She fit into the high-profile structure of his life because she'd been groomed almost from birth to marry someone of wealth.

Educated? Check. She had a masters in art history from UC Berkeley.

Poise, charm, and grace? Check. She understood business protocol and the norms for any number of social engagements.

The right background? Check. Her mother, now deceased, had been a model for a few years and her father had made a fortune in commercial real estate before selling his company and retiring to Florida. There were no embarrassing scandals in her past, and like his family, hers could trace their roots back for generations.

"Should I be flattered you chose me and were willing to spend an exorbitant amount of money to get me to marry you?"

"You could be, but I suspect that you aren't." He watched her closely, like the shark he was, likely trying to determine what her next move would be, but he had no idea.

She turned away so he wouldn't see the pain in her face. Cyrus was good at reading people, and it hadn't been easy to keep her true feelings from him for fear he would use them against her. The stress had taken its toll, and now finding out what he'd done only deepened her distrust of him.

"You're not sorry at all for what you did, are you?" she asked.

"My only regret is trusting that snake, Roland DuBois, to keep his mouth shut. Frankly Dani, you should be thanking me for getting him out of your life. You needed someone stronger."

She swung back around. "Someone like you, maybe? A control freak who bullies people into doing what he wants them to?" Cyrus didn't concern himself with other people's wants or needs. All that mattered was what he wanted.

"He didn't deserve you," he said, as if he hadn't heard a word she'd said. "What did you ever see in him, anyway—a wannabe entrepreneur in off-the-rack suits."

"For goodness's sake, Cyrus, not everyone can afford Brioni." Every suit and tuxedo he owned was handmade by the designer.

"True." He looked so smug.

"You're such an ass."

He smiled, an unapologetic Master-of-the-Universe smile. The same one that had captured her attention from the beginning and still managed to make her abdomen contract in unwavering attraction. "Yeah, but you like it."

A thread of acknowledgement went through her at the truth of his words. She did like the strength he exuded and the power he wielded. Perhaps too much. They were sexy traits for sure, and being with a man like him was exciting, until you saw the ugly side of his power. He manipulated people and situations. His actions made old wounds resurface—wounds she'd tried to heal for years but hadn't been able to.

"I'm a better man than Roland DuBois—" he said the name with a curl of his lips "—could ever dream of being. I'm a man of my word, and I'll continue to make sure you have everything you could ever want or need."

Everything, every material possession imaginable was hers if she asked. She fingered her diamond choker. It suddenly felt like a noose, one she'd willingly slipped around her own neck. How could she continue to live with him, knowing he'd blackmailed Roland out of her life? One of his many transgressions, too many to name.

"This changes everything."

He watched her without flinching. Emotionless. Unfeeling. "For now."

"For good."

He rose slowly from the chair. "You're upset," he said. "Once you calm down you'll rethink what you've said."

She hated the way he always made her sound so unreasonable, as if he was the only one who exemplified logic and common sense. "No, I won't. I'm thinking clearly right now, and I won't forget what you did. It's over. I can't trust you, and I never will." She pivoted away from him.

"Divorce is not an option," he said, halting her in her tracks. He hadn't raised his voice a single decibel. How could he sound so calm in the middle of a monumental argument? She wanted to scream.

She whirled to face him again. "Do you really think you can hold onto me if I want to leave?" she asked, incredulous.

His eyes were as hard as steel. One would think *she* had done something wrong. "You can leave whenever you want, Dani. I won't hold you against your will. That would be a monstrous thing to do."

"And everyone knows you're not a monster," she said sarcastically.

He began to remove his gold cuff links. Slowly, he slipped each piece of jewelry between its buttonhole. She'd bought them for him, each one monogrammed with his initials, CJ. "You made me a promise, and I expect you to keep it."

She couldn't believe he'd brought up the conversation they'd had weeks ago. She laughed, the sound shrill and unnatural. "Don't hold your breath."

He didn't react. If he'd given any indication this argument affected him nearly as much as it did her, perhaps they'd have stood a chance, but her husband rarely expressed emotion. Strict control in his life was paramount at all times, and he actually became even more detached during their arguments.

"Our marriage is over, Cyrus." She didn't move, temporarily paralyzed by the magnitude of her decision. Saying the words made it final. She would no longer wrestle with the decision in her head because she'd put it out there in the universe. She'd told him and fully intended to carry through with her decision, no matter how much it pained her. "One of these days someone will deceive you, too, and we'll see how you like it."

His silence was unbearable. Since he didn't respond to her warning, she left him alone to enter the main area of their bedroom. He came up behind her, as stealthy as a big cat, and caught her by the arm. Pushing her back against the wall, he leaned close and barricaded her in with hands on either side of her body.

"Stay away from Roland DuBois," he said, low and succinct. "If I ever find out he's made contact with you again, *I will destroy him.*" He paused to let the words sink in.

Her heart tripped in her chest. Cyrus didn't make idle threats.

His eyes lowered to the bodice of her dress, which dipped low and exposed her full cleavage. He'd bought it for her, a one-of-a-kind Alexander McQueen. The golden lamé sparkled against her light caramel complexion and fit her figure perfectly. She'd had to admit it was a good choice, and by the look in his eyes, she knew that as much as he liked to see her in it, now Cyrus wanted her out of it as quickly as possible.

She shrank back against the wall, seeking distance between them but finding none.

"Are we done?" she asked. Unable to tolerate being in the same room with him for another minute, she had every intention of spending the night in one of the spare bedrooms on the other side of the house, as far away from him as possible.

"No, we're not done." The words dripped slowly from his lips like warm, heavy syrup. "Time to go to bed." His head dipped to hers and she immediately placed her hands against his broad shoulders to shove him away. Instead of letting her go, he scooped her up and carried her to their large bed.

Pinning her arms above her head, he kissed her the way he wanted to. Slowly, thoroughly. He loved to kiss, and he was extremely good at it. The seductive movements of his lips over hers battered her resistance.

"Don't fight me," he said against her cheek.

He ran one hand down the inside of her arm, over her breasts and down to her hip. She twisted and arched, the heat of his touch warming her skin through the material. Already he had her wanting more.

Cupping one breast, he kissed the line of her cleavage and pulled in frustration at the edge of the gown, seeking her nipple. In his impatience, he ripped the dress down the middle, a dress that had cost him thousands. Daniella gasped.

"I'll buy you another one," he said. He licked the tips of her breasts, unleashing a pool of heat in her belly. "I'll buy you a thousand more," he said to the underside of her breast. His voice was rough with hunger, and the sound of it was like an aphrodisiac.

He reached lower. The gold thong was torn from her hips like a thin layer of tissue, his fingers anxious, his chest heaving with each labored breath.

He pressed her legs apart, and when his face disappeared between her thighs, she let loose a whimper of surrender. She'd long ago recognized she couldn't refuse him. It had always been like this between them—a fiery passion that burned everything in its path and left her trembling, throbbing, and at his mercy.

As his mouth moved over her tender flesh, she closed her eyes and forgot their argument, concentrated on the caress of his lips and tongue, and temporarily shelved any thought of leaving him.

CHAPTER TWO

Present day

Cyrus entered his suite of offices after his normal one hour workout in the company gym. He'd been in since before six. Roxanne, his executive assistant, who made sure she was available whenever he arrived from his workout, greeted him. A tall black woman, she had a no-nonsense set to her mouth, no matter the occasion.

"Good morning, Mr. Johnson." She pushed her funky fuchsia glasses higher on her nose. They might have looked out of place on an older woman, but they didn't on Roxanne. She'd worked for his father when he was alive, and from what Cyrus had heard, she'd been quite the hellion in her day.

"Hardy called you back and said he's available whenever you are," she said, following him into his office and reading from an electronic tablet in her hand.

"He'd better be." Hardy Malcomb worked out of their London office and oversaw beer production in western Europe. Cyrus hadn't been pleased to learn production levels had dropped because of bad hops they'd purchased, which meant they couldn't meet production schedules and supplier demand.

He took a bottle of water from the small refrigerator under the bar in his office. He kept the bar stocked with the finest spirits to entertain guests, but he didn't drink—not even the beer his family brewed. He hadn't had anything alcoholic since his father passed away at the hands of a drunk driver.

Ironically, the man who'd killed his father had empty cans of Full Moon beer—the Johnson family brew—strewn on the floor of his vehicle. He'd been working on emptying another one when he plowed into the car carrying Cyrus's father and his brother, Gavin.

"A reporter from the *Seattle Business Chronicle* called and wanted to interview you about the upswing in sales and what you think it's attributed to."

Cyrus emptied the bottle and tossed it in the trash. He retrieved another and swallowed a gulp of cool water before responding. "Let Trenton talk to the reporter." Although Cyrus had been closely involved in the changes to their marketing strategy, his brother ran the Sales and Marketing division and should be the one to discuss the ideas they'd implemented. Besides, he was much better at schmoozing the press, a task Cyrus considered a chore.

Roxanne nodded and left his office. Cyrus pulled his sweaty T-shirt over his head and went through the door that led to a full private bathroom and dressing area. After a quick shower, he changed into one of five suits hanging in the closet. Today he chose black with a white shirt and navy tie.

He then had Roxanne call Hardy and pass the call through to him. The conversation went downhill within a few minutes.

"Saying 'I'm doing my best' is not an answer." Squeezing a tension ball in his hand, Cyrus paced in front of the cherry wood desk in his office. "Your job is to make sure we produce enough beer to satisfy the market. If your best allows us to fall below quota so we're scrambling to meet orders, that, Hardy, is not good enough."

Hardy Malcomb had been with the company for many years, but right now he was skating on thin ice.

"Cyrus, with all due respect, your father—"

"My father has been dead for almost ten years." Cyrus stopped pacing and leaned over the phone so Hardy heard everything he said next, including the hard note in his voice. The comparisons to his father, Cyrus Senior, had gotten old long ago, and Hardy should know better. His father had never tolerated mediocre performance, and neither would he. "I'm the one in charge, and it would behoove you to find out what's going on. I'll be keeping a close eye on production levels moving forward, and if I don't see an improvement, you'll have a major problem on your hands. Get it done, or I'll find someone who can. Have I made myself clear?"

There was a prolonged silence before the man spoke again. "Yes, I understand," he said in a defeated voice.

"I don't want to have another one of these conversations, Hardy. It wastes your time as well as mine. Have a good day."

Cyrus jabbed the intercom button and disconnected the call. He hated having to deal with something as simple as quotas first thing in the morning. He hadn't even bothered to have breakfast sent up because he'd wanted to tackle this problem right away. Production levels had fallen well below the norm. If they didn't hit those numbers, they couldn't fill orders, and if they couldn't fill orders, they lost money. As if he didn't already have enough on his plate with a possible trademark infringement from a small brewery in Canada and the equipment failure at their facility in Portland.

Cyrus rolled his shoulders and tried to release the tension, to no avail. He was a man of routine. It kept him on track, but since he'd missed breakfast, his routine was off, and tension settled in his neck and shoulders.

He'd hoped the day would progress more smoothly moving forward, but luck was not with him. At least not by the sound of the raised voices coming from outside his office. He strode to the closed door and opened it to see Roxanne in a heated argument with his wife,

Daniella.

He came to a complete stop.

The sight of her stole every molecule of air from his lungs and temporarily left him without the ability to breathe. He couldn't remember the last time she'd visited the company—more than two years at least.

As usual she dressed like the goddess she was in a black, short-sleeved jumpsuit with wide legs. A thin gold belt brought attention to her narrow waistline, and manicured toes covered in polish the same color of a natural pearl were on display in a pair of three-inch sandals that matched the belt.

Her eyes lifted to his and he clenched a fist to fight back the instantaneous tightening of his abdominal muscles.

"Cyrus, do you mind calling off your secretary?" She looked pointedly at Roxanne, who still blocked her path to his doorway.

"She's doing her job," he replied.

"Her job is to keep me out?"

"Her job is to make sure I'm not disturbed. I'm a busy man, and all kinds of random people like to come here and disrupt my day." He leaned a shoulder against the door and folded his arms.

Her tawny cheeks blushed the color of fully ripe peaches. "I'm not a random person, I'm your wife." True, but she'd been fighting to change her status.

"Roxanne, you can let her by, and while I'm with my *wife*, please make sure we're not interrupted."

"Yes, sir." Roxanne stepped aside. She took her job seriously, which made her indispensable to him. If he said he didn't want to be disturbed, Jesus Christ and a host of angels couldn't get past her without an appointment.

Daniella cast a scathing look in the older woman's direction before lifting her head high and stalking by. She traipsed past Cyrus with a stiff spine, and he followed more slowly.

He closed the door.

"To what do I owe this visit? It's been what—a year? Two years, since I've seen you?" Not since the opening of a restaurant by mutual friends, and he knew exactly how long ago that had been.

"A year, but it went by so fast. I guess that's what happens when you enjoy your freedom and have fun," she said.

Her cutting remark only made him smile. "You wouldn't know what fun is if it jumped up and bit you on the nose."

They both shunned the typical trappings of entertainment that bludgeoned less focused people. He and Daniella were both goal-oriented and driven. Those characteristics should have helped their marriage work, but the cracks in their union had widened into valleys they couldn't bridge.

He gestured at the guest chair. "Have a seat."

"I'd rather stand."

"Suit yourself."

Cyrus settled into the high-backed chair behind his desk and observed her in more detail. She'd always been thin, although she appeared to be even more so now, and he wondered if she was taking care of herself. Whenever she worked hard, she tended to forego meals, grabbing a snack here and there, which he'd told her on numerous occasions was not healthy. At the pace she kept, it was important to fuel her body.

What she lacked in curves she made up for with breasts the size of cantaloupes. They were magnificent—the only word he could think of to describe them—and large enough to seem out of place on her slender body. His gaze dipped to them and he suffered the expected consequences. His groin tightened and his mouth watered. No doubt about it, they were his favorite part of her anatomy.

"I wouldn't be here, except you won't accept my calls," she explained.

He lifted his gaze to her face. Her hair was parted in the middle but pulled back with gold clips. He'd always felt the hairstyle made her look too severe because of her pointy chin and high cheekbones. He preferred when she wore it straight or wavy and allowed the lustrous strands to soften her face and frame her delicate features.

"What could you possibly want to talk to me about?" He crossed his legs and leaned back in the chair, pretending to be relaxed when in fact her appearance had made him more tense than he was before. "You were the one who said everything we needed to say could be communicated between our lawyers."

"That's what I prefer."

"Well then, what's the problem? I take it you've changed your mind?"

"Obviously, Cyrus, but as usual, you have to be difficult." She walked forward, carefully, as if approaching an undomesticated animal and she didn't know how it would respond to her overtures. "I came because I want a divorce."

"That would be obvious from the divorce papers you served me with. I haven't forgotten." His gaze shifted to the purse she held in front of her. She wasn't wearing her rings, and the sight of her bare finger pissed him off.

"It's been three years. Now you've petitioned the court to dismiss the divorce completely. You're unnecessarily dragging out the process."

"Unnecessary for you, but necessary for me."

"Cyrus, it's time we end this."

"End what?"

"End *this*. The back and forth, this marriage neither of us wants."

"Where is this coming from?" he asked. To his knowledge, nothing had changed recently.

"I'm tired of fighting you. What you really want is to win, so I've come to make you an offer. Tell me what you need to be crowned the victor. Whatever it is, I'll give it to you." She took small steps forward, and despite her outward calm, the harsh grip on her purse betrayed her agitation. Had it been a neck she would have snapped it for sure. "I'll leave with whatever I came into the marriage with and you can have everything else, even what's due me in the prenup. I'll walk away with nothing I didn't earn myself."

Any other man would be ecstatic his wife made divorce so easy, but her words pushed another button and brought him that much closer to anger. His neck muscles tightened.

Cyrus rested his elbow on the arm of the chair. "You don't want anything else?"

"That's right," she assured him. "Nothing."

"I'm afraid I can't just let you walk away," he said.

"Why not?" The desperation in her voice scraped the air like nails on soft flesh. "I don't want anything—not the cars or the jewelry. Nothing. You can have it all back."

"Those were gifts," he said quietly. Her willingness to give up all he'd given her, to cut her losses and get out of their marriage, burned his stomach. While she earned a comfortable living, his degree of wealth had exposed her to a lifestyle most people only dreamed about. Her dismissal was nothing more than an insult.

"I'll give it all back if you sign."

"You know the situation is not that simple, Dani."

"It can be. Would it help if I withdrew?" She sounded more and more desperate. Desperate to get away from him. "You could divorce me, instead. I don't care. Just...let me go, Cyrus. I can't fight you anymore."

He lifted one shoulder in a shrug. "Then stop fighting and come home."

"Come home to what?" She huffed in exasperation. "There's nothing there for me."

He was there, but obviously she didn't see him as much of an incentive.

"Then this conversation is over." He turned his attention to the financial reports displayed on the computer screen in front of him. He had way too much work to do to waste any more time on this ridiculous argument.

"I won't beg you."

"I never asked you to beg," he said, talking to the screen on his desk. He checked the variance column and used the cursor to highlight a budget item with a twenty-three percent increase over the previous year. Then he waved his hand dismissively toward the door. "See yourself out."

"Cyrus." He shielded his conscience from the pleading tone of her voice. She took a deep breath. "Think about this for a minute. Your behavior is keeping us both from moving on and being happy. If we end our marriage, we'd be free to find other spouses, people we're more compatible with."

He paid closer attention to her now.

Was that it? Had she met someone? His brain recoiled at the thought, and anger raged anew inside him. She thought she could get a divorce so she could run into someone else's arms? Not a chance.

"I'm done talking," he said coldly.

"Cyrus."

He shot to his feet and she jerked back at the sudden movement. Pressing his hands on the surface of the desk, he leaned toward her. "The answer is no." He kept his voice even, but firm.

"You can't keep me tied to you forever!" Her eyes flashed in anger.

"Marriage is a contract."

"Any contract can be broken," she retorted.

"You want to break the contract of our marriage? You want a divorce?" he seethed. "Give me what I want. And you know what I want."

Her eyes widened in disbelief. They were a striking brown color—

copper, the same tint as a shiny new penny. "You can't be serious."

"You know I never say anything I don't mean."

"You black-hearted bastard."

"Flatter me all you want. The answer is the same."

"You were serious? You can't possibly expect me to—"

"I do."

The color drained from her face, and she stepped back from the desk, shunning his words.

"Give me a child, Dani, and I'll give you a divorce."

Chapter Three

Daniella knew her husband could be unreasonable, but this was too much even for him. He was mad. Completely and utterly off his rocker.

Yes, he'd told her he wanted a child, preferably a son. An heir he could groom to carry on the Johnson name and take his rightful place at the helm of the company, the same way he had done. But after so much time apart, she didn't think he would still demand the same from her. She'd hoped she could reason with him, but he remained as ruthless and irrational as ever.

His coffee-colored eyes bored into hers, and his face, handsome by anyone's standards, was set in arrogant, unyielding lines that made it clear this one point was nonnegotiable. The angular planes were offset by a pair of lips that were sensual in design and soft to the touch. She almost shuddered at the memory of how those lips could make her unravel.

"We haven't lived together as husband and wife in a long time."

"Refusing to wear your rings and live in our house doesn't make you any less my wife."

Her eyes dropped to his fingers splayed out on the desk. He still wore his ring, a platinum band custom designed to match her engagement and wedding rings. The fact he still wore the jewelry, the symbol of their union, didn't surprise her. Cyrus had never accepted their marriage was over.

She'd spent the last few years fighting to be free of him, but they weren't any closer to the termination of their marriage than when she'd started the process. He'd told her he wouldn't give her a divorce, and she'd disregarded his resolve, believing—no, hoping—once the proceedings started he would see she was serious and give in. But she'd learned the hard way that he truly never said anything he didn't mean.

The first year after she'd left him, she'd thought they were simply ironing out the details. Her lawyer had assured her the time frame was typical, but halfway through year two she realized Cyrus had no intention of ending their relationship, no matter her concessions. Even his travel schedule had been used as an excuse to prolong the process. He had an infinite amount of funds at his disposal, and he used his money to pay a team of lawyers to create constant delays, filing motion after motion and requests for evidence to keep her chained to him.

"What you're suggesting will never happen," she said.

"If that's your final answer, then as I said before, we're done talking, aren't we?"

"This is insane!" Daniella exclaimed. "How do you expect me to give you a child?"

"Do I really need to explain the birds and the bees to you?" he asked. "I thought I'd done a pretty good job already of showing you how the male and female anatomy worked together. Do you need a refresher?"

The flutter of her stomach testified to how her body managed to betray her time and time again. His voice had lowered to a silky timbre and brought back memories of constantly making love, where sleep and food were unwelcome interruptions, and the only sustenance she craved came from his drugging kisses and tender caresses. His eyes held a possessive gleam as they drifted over her. She fought back the sensual images creeping to the perimeter of her mind and the unwanted throb manifesting between her thighs—a not-so-subtle reminder that when they made love, almost nothing was off-limits.

"No, I don't need a refresher," she said huskily.

She told herself her undeniable attraction to him was because he was her first and only lover. She'd waited much longer than most to explore sex because she'd been focused on academic achievements. She'd continued to hold out, despite the ribbing incurred from friends and the unrelenting efforts of boyfriends to wear her down over the years. But she'd had her eyes on the prize of success, and nothing— especially not a man—would deter her from achieving her goals. In her own home she'd seen the result of dreams deferred, and she'd decided years ago she would not fall prey to the unrealistic romantic ideas of happily ever after.

Yet she'd been intensely attracted to him from their first introduction. Unnervingly so. Who wouldn't be? Indecently good looking, he carried himself with a level of confidence she'd never encountered in any other man. It wasn't only the way he walked or his movements. It was the sound of his voice, the beauty of his smooth, dark brown skin, his full lips, and the intense way he always looked at her as if no one else was around. But at the time she'd been involved with someone else, Roland Dubois, though it hadn't been a love match. She'd told Cyrus about her relationship, beating back his aggressive tactics to win her over—which hadn't been easy.

Even with her lack of experience, she knew her body's response to him had less to do with him being her first and more to do with his skills as a lover. Sex with him had transcended mere physical pleasure, bordering on the spiritual, and had always left her spent and in a euphoric state afterward.

To hide the truth from his probing gaze, Daniella stared down at her hands. Noting the stranglehold on her purse, she loosened her grip. She had to make him understand they couldn't possibly bring a child into the world and then simply divorce.

To prove her own fortitude in the face of his unyielding strength, she edged forward, her thighs touching his desk. "What you're suggesting is unconscionable. Why are you doing this?"

"Shouldn't I get something out of this marriage?" he asked roughly.

His question surprised her. It meant he believed he had been shortchanged—that she had not held up her end of the marriage deal, which was untrue. She'd done her part. He was the one who'd changed the rules and expected her to fall in line with his plans.

"You expect me to have a baby with you and then walk away?" She couldn't quell the note of hysteria in her voice.

"I've told you what I want."

"And what about what I want? Can't you find someone else to do this for you?" There were numerous women who would gladly give birth to a Johnson heir. During the brief time they dated, she'd seen how mothers and fathers practically tossed their daughters at his feet. Even after they married, the same behavior continued, though not as flagrantly. The parents at least took into account if she was standing beside him.

"I'm not going to keep arguing with you about the same thing. I won't change. If all you want to do is argue, you can leave now."

He sat down and returned his eyes to the screen, effectively dismissing her. For him, the conversation was over, because that's how he operated. He'd laid out what he wanted and expected her to simply fall in line with his plans.

His gaze remained on the laptop. She stared at his profile, his hard, clean-shaven jaw and hair cut low on his head. He wore a Brioni suit in the darkest black with a navy blue tie and matching handkerchief sticking out the left pocket. Immaculate. Always.

He didn't look at her, and his lack of interest pushed her over the edge. She wanted to unsettle him, the same as he'd done to her. Short of smashing one of the desk organizers over his head, she couldn't think of any nonviolent way to disturb him except one.

She cast her eyes across his neatly arranged desk. Everything in its place. He was obsessive about it, a man of routine and discipline. Three pens were lined up across the top, perpendicular to the edge of the desk. One black. One blue. One red. A cylindrical container held his letter opener, highlighters, a pencil, and two more pens. A leather bound notepad sat in the middle of the desk.

She snatched up the blue pen from the desk and his eyes snapped to her. She had his attention now.

"What are you doing, Dani? Put that down."

"Your answer is no and so is mine," she said. She used the blue pen to knock the other two askew.

Cyrus jumped up from the chair. His flesh must be crawling now because she'd disrupted his orderly life. As he rounded the desk, she dropped the pen to the floor and grabbed the letter opener. She pulled it with such force the glass container tipped over and scattered pens and highlighters across the desk.

"Get back," she said, holding the letter opener above her head as a weapon.

"Put that down. You're not going to use it." He sounded bored.

"Yes, I will." Her voice trembled, but she tightened her grip on the chrome handle. "Get away from me," she warned.

"Or what? You'll stab me?" He spoke in a calm voice, completely unfazed by her dramatic display. He took a step and she took one back. "Violence is ugly on you, Dani. I like you so much better when you're under me, gasping and purring from pleasure."

Memories—unwelcome and sudden—flashed through her mind, triggering a delicious heat in her loins. How could he do this to her even when she was angry at him?

"Let me go, Cyrus. Please." She'd said she wouldn't beg, told herself so many times, but she couldn't fight him anymore. She was tired and frantic and spending way too much money on something that should have ended long ago.

"Give me a child and I'll let you go."

He took another step forward and she took another one back.

She shook her head.

His hand whipped out and snagged her wrist. He held her firm without hurting her, but she knew he could. He was twice her size and she couldn't match his strength.

She twisted her arm, but with another quick, deft motion, he snatched the weapon from her fingers and tossed it onto the desk. It clattered against the polished wood, and she gasped in dismay at how easily he'd disarmed her.

Cyrus yanked her closer until barely an inch of charged air remained between them. The subtle scent of $165-per-ounce cologne filled her nostrils. Spicy, with an undertone of citrus, it was his signature smell—a scent she'd once equated with passion. The fragrance lingered in his clothes, and there had been times when she'd worn his shirts around the house so she could savor the scent of him while he was away on business. Her own little secret.

His eyes held dark determination as he looked down at her from several inches above six feet. His other hand circled the back of her neck, applying a warm, firm pressure. Years had passed since he last touched her, and she shivered in his grip. His thumb rubbed the tender spot behind her ear, and heat flashed over her skin. She had to remind herself the purpose of his touch was not to awaken desire in her. He was angry.

He lowered his head and his breath skimmed her lips. Her skin tingled as they breathed the same air, and she thought for sure he was about to kiss her. Could she possibly resist him? Fear of her reaction overwhelmed her, and she trembled with anticipation, but the kiss never came.

"You can beg, you can fight, you can threaten me all you want," he all but snarled, all civility gone. His lips were held so close together she only caught a glimpse of his teeth. "But I want a child, just like you promised. And you're going to give it to me." His jaw firmed and his eyes filled with angry resolve. "I'm not letting you go until you do."

CHAPTER FOUR

Daniella tugged free of his grasp, clearly shaken at the nature of his request. They stared at each other. She was breathing heavily, and if he knew his wife—which he did—her shallow breathing was not solely due to anger. No, she was as aroused as he was.

He reminded her of the conversation they'd had years ago. "You said you didn't want to have a child right away. That we should wait a few years before we tried. Do you remember?"

At first, a confused frown creased her brow. Then it disappeared as she recalled the conversation. "I said that, but before we decided to get a divorce."

"Before *you* decided you wanted to divorce me. You made an offer and I accepted. Three years. Now I want what you promised."

"No way." She shook her head.

"No?" he asked with a raised eyebrow.

"*No,*" she said adamantly.

He shrugged and walked back around his desk. He sank into the seat. "How's Roland these days?" he asked. She didn't respond, eyeing him with suspicion. As well she should. "Don't pretend you haven't seen him. I know all about your little meeting."

"Are you spying on me?" she demanded.

"I'm spying on him."

"What for?"

"I have my reasons." He chose not to elaborate. He didn't want to tip his hand, but Roland DuBois would pay for what he had done.

"What are you up to?" she asked.

"You're not getting a divorce, Dani," he replied, dodging the question. "You might as well accept it."

"Then I'll keep fighting you."

"I look forward to it."

She swallowed. "You can't keep this up forever."

"No?" He allowed a small smile to lift the corner of his mouth. "Who do you think will run out of money first?"

She shook her head in disbelief. He could only imagine the names she called him in her head. "You…" At a loss for words, she swung around and marched toward the door.

"Have a nice day," Cyrus couldn't resist calling out to her.

Daniella paused and sent one last scorching look over her shoulder at him before yanking open the door. Had she emitted a little more force, she would have torn it in half. She swept through like a tornado and slammed the door shut.

Alone now, Cyrus lifted his right thumb to his nose and inhaled the scent of her perfume. The light, sweet fragrance of pomegranate greeted his nostrils. She'd always dotted perfume behind her ears and freshened the scent throughout the day. Clearly she continued to do the same.

He went around the desk and picked up the blue pen she'd discarded to the floor and put everything back into place on the wooden surface. Then he walked over to the huge windows and looked down at the bustling city.

He shouldn't feel so good about their confrontation, but her anger, her passion, her fight excited him. His blood was pumping and his pulse worked overtime. Damn, he missed her. Seeing her, *touching* her, had brought it home. From the moment he'd met her, he hadn't been able to get her out of his mind, and he'd decided right away she would become his wife. He'd even told her so, but she'd laughed at his forwardness.

Women weren't the only ones who made life plans. Years ago a health scare had forced him to think about his own mortality. It had reminded him of the fleeting nature of life and his father's last days after his accident. Cyrus Senior had been a big man with a big voice. He'd dominated any room he entered and ran his company with an iron fist, but the last time Cyrus had seen him, the vibrancy had left his body and he lay dying in a hospital bed.

Cyrus's mother had been asleep on the sofa in the private room, a blanket thrown over her legs as she slept. She hadn't left her husband's side since he'd entered the hospital.

His father had lain there, wasting away, a shadow of his former self. He'd looked at Cyrus from the hospital bed, his voice raspy as he drew his last breaths and delivered his final instructions.

With all the money they had, they hadn't been able to save him. The internal injuries had been too severe, and in the end, after numerous surgeries, his heart had finally given way under the strain. Would his father have lived if he'd exercised more and eaten better? If he'd taken better care of himself, could he have withstood the trauma?

With those events buoying his decision-making, Cyrus had mapped out a new life for himself. He'd bought a house with the intention of getting married and starting a family by the age of thirty-two. Yet here he was at thirty-four years old and not a child in sight.

Plenty of potential wives had crossed his path, but he hadn't had time to date, so he'd hired a high-end dating service to find him a spouse. Around the same time, Johnson Enterprises had been going through a redecoration. Daniella's company, Beaux-Arts Galleries, had met with their facilities manager to work on the new decor. He'd only needed to meet her once to know she was the right woman, and a background check had confirmed it. There had been no skeletons in her closet.

After he'd gotten rid of her boyfriend, Roland, they'd connected easily because they understood each other's work ethic. Their courtship had been short, but established they were compatible enough to get along, and then they'd been married. A strong attraction to each other helped, but the marriage itself had been a practical matter, without the emotional trappings of declarations of love. More or less a business arrangement that fit their lifestyles and happened to extend into the bedroom.

They'd enjoyed a few good months of marriage when he noticed the change in her. That's when the problems started. Some days she simply watched him, her eyes filled with reproof. Other times, she questioned his business decisions, the way he treated members of his family, and the tactics he used to get the outcomes he desired. Rather than getting better, their arguments escalated. Not a surprise, considering both he and Daniella were stubborn.

None of that mattered. She was his wife, and now the allotted time had passed, he expected her to follow through on her promise to give him a child.

****

Daniella walked briskly past Roxanne and down the hallway toward the elevators that would get her out of the building and away from Cyrus. She didn't say a word to the receptionist she passed in the main lobby of the executive floor. She stabbed the elevator button and waited, blinking back tears of frustration.

He was a Neanderthal. He was a selfish prick.

She wished there was someone she could call and complain to, but his request—no, his demand—was too outrageous, and she had trouble digesting the enormity of it. Even though right before they'd separated he'd told her he wanted a child, she hadn't believed he was serious. Now she knew how serious he was. How could she possibly explain his angry ultimatum to anyone?

There was no way she was going to have a baby because he said so. He could hold his damn breath until he turned purple.

She rode the elevator to the atrium on the first floor, relieved the erratic beat of her heart had lessened to a slower pace. Her brisk walk slowed as she neared her white CL-Class Mercedes coupe in the parking garage.

With her brain no longer smothered in frustration and what she unwillingly admitted had been panic, she could think clearly.

"I want children, and I need a wife," he'd told her what seemed like ages ago.

As proposals went, it was tragically unromantic, but she'd said yes. For the most part, they wanted the same thing out of marriage—companionship. Combined with a mutual respect, it had been sufficient. Her parents had proven love didn't mean you'd have a happy marriage. The whole sordid story of how her parents' relationship fell apart was never far from her mind.

She'd wanted children, too, like Cyrus, but not on the same timeline. She'd had plans to expand her gallery which, true enough, she'd done over the past few years. Now she was on the brink of opening a storefront in New York. Even if she considered his demand—which she wasn't about to—she simply didn't have time to devote to a child. Not when she would be pulled in numerous directions in the coming months.

She stewed on the problem. Cyrus had the financial means to drag out the divorce indefinitely, and he was hell bent on doing so. She knew of at least one divorce battle that had lasted for ten years! There was no way in hell she was going to fight him for that long. If she was to get out of this relationship, she had to force his hand. But how? He wouldn't change, and the more she fought him, the harder he dug in his heels.

Daniella entered her car and sat there for awhile, thinking.

Cyrus's comment about Roland made her uneasy. She and Roland had stayed away from each other after her separation from her husband. Partly because of Cyrus's warning, but mostly because she'd felt betrayed by her ex.

But a month ago Roland had made an unexpected visit to her gallery. According to him, he'd dropped by to say hi and see how she was doing. He'd apologized profusely for his role in her deception and said he wanted to be friends. She'd put him off, not sure she wanted him in her life again, because though he'd come clean, she'd been disappointed he'd taken the million dollars from Cyrus.

As she pulled out of the parking deck, she called her attorney, Davis Williams, the one person she could talk to and trust. "I need to talk to you. Are you free?"

"Can you come now?" he asked.

"I'll be there in ten minutes."

His building was located nearby, and soon enough she'd parked on the street and was headed up in the elevator to his office. She'd known Davis for years. He'd been a friend of her mother's and had handled her parents' divorce when she was a child. After her mother's death, he'd ensured the proceeds from her life insurance policy had been administered according to her wishes. Thanks to the payout from the policy and other items of value her mother had left her, she'd been able to live comfortably and start her own business.

Daniella entered Davis's office. Gray peppered his receding hairline at the temples, and he smiled behind his glasses, motioning for her to have a seat.

"I can't sit," she said, still a little agitated. She set her purse on the chair and paced the room, giving him a quick rundown of her conversation with Cyrus. Davis's eyebrows elevated.

Daniella stopped pacing long enough to look at her attorney. "There's got to be a way to get me out of this marriage." She continued her restless walk across his office. "He's impossible."

Davis cleared his throat before speaking. "You know what we're up against. Have you considered…" His voice trailed off when her head snapped in his direction.

"Don't even think about it," she said. This wasn't the first time Davis had hinted she should consider a reconciliation with Cyrus.

"Why not? I'm running out of ideas, and clearly he wants to stay married. Quite unusual, frankly." He said the last under his breath.

"I don't care what he wants."

"Well, you should, because the only thing he seems to want is you."

"And a baby," Daniella reminded him. She sighed dramatically. "He doesn't want me, really. He wants to control me. Anyone who would buy another man's debts to gain leverage over him…" She shook her head. "If I have a child with Cyrus, who knows what tactics he'll pull next. The next thing I know, he'll end up taking over my business and forcing me to be a stay-at-home mother. No." She shook her head vehemently. This was not an option for her. "There's got to be another way."

"There is one thing we haven't tried, but it's risky."

"What?" Eager, Daniella rushed over to his desk.

Davis raised his hands to calm her down. "It's just a thought, but the Johnsons are extremely protective about their public image. They have public relations people whose sole responsibility is to manage media relations and keep their names out of the tabloids—as much as possible, anyway."

She understood why he'd added the qualifier at the end. The media often sought out information about the Johnsons because of their unique position. They owned one of the largest brewing companies in the country—in the world, even—and not only was it still privately owned, as an African-American family, their staggering wealth was an oddity in the beer industry.

Davis leaned forward and folded his hands. "We could do a little reconnaissance and see if he's been involved with anyone. If he has a mistress or girlfriend of any sort, we could use it as leverage in the divorce proceedings, and we could easily leak the information to the press and let the court of public opinion push this to a resolution once and for all. Having him force you to stay married while he's off with another woman would not reflect positively on him."

One hand on her hip, Daniella raised her other hand to her mouth and bit down on her finger. She didn't like the idea. It seemed like a dirty thing to do, but what choice did she have? She'd have to fight fire with fire.

Before she could argue herself out of a perfectly viable idea, she nodded, swallowing. "Do you have an investigator in mind?"

"I do. Let me handle everything, and I'll let you know how it goes."

Daniella nodded again, a feeling of nausea bubbling up in the pit of her stomach at the steps she was being forced to take. "I better go," she said. "Give me an update next week?"

"Sure will."

She picked up her purse and crossed the room.

"Daniella?"

She halted at the door.

"Don't worry, kiddo. It'll work out. At least you're in a better position than your mother was."

"Yeah, lucky me."

In the elevator, Daniella leaned against the wall. True enough, she was in a much better position than her mother had been. She didn't have a child and she had her own business, both very important factors in life-after-Cyrus. Her mother had been convinced to give up her modeling career to start a family with a man who not long after abandoned her for another woman. He'd manipulated her into going along with his choices, tricked her into a false sense of security, and then left her.

At least he'd paid child support, Daniella thought bitterly.

She hadn't seen her father in years. Not since he sold his real estate business and moved to Florida with his new family.

She jabbed the button for the first floor in anger, even though it was already lit.

Taking a deep breath, she closed her eyes and tried to calm down. Davis was right. She wouldn't be like her mother, which was a good thing. Except...she took another deep breath. What if Cyrus did have a woman in his life?

It shouldn't matter after all this time. Not once in the past three years had she seen him linked with anyone else in the press, but that didn't mean he wasn't seeing someone. Maybe he was simply careful.

She rubbed the spot behind her ear where he'd touched her and her heart did a little quiver.

She'd done good to stay away from him for so long, but what choice did she have? He made her feel nervous, excited, and weak all at the same time. Weakness was the most dangerous of those sensations. Being weak made you vulnerable. Once you were vulnerable, you could be hurt deeply. Irrevocably.

No one should have so much power over another.

CHAPTER FIVE

A week passed and Daniella didn't hear from Cyrus, which suited her fine. It had taken a few days to recover from the confrontation with him anyway. Going to see him had been a lapse in judgment.

During a phone call with Davis a few days ago, he'd given her good news that the investigator had already started tailing Cyrus. She hoped he would have something of substance soon—some dirt she could use to force his hand.

In the meantime, she planned to forget her problems and enjoy a meal out. Roland had invited her out to dinner and she'd accepted.

At first she'd declined, worried Cyrus might have eyes everywhere. She'd even warned Roland that her husband knew they'd met once before, but he appeared unconcerned.

When she entered The Savory Date, a Moroccan restaurant and her absolute favorite place to eat, the inviting scent of savory stews simmering in spices greeted her and created a spike in her appetite. She hadn't been eating well, a common condition when she worked long hours. If Cyrus knew, he wouldn't be pleased and would make her get food in her stomach. He'd done it several times, bringing her a meal on his way somewhere and forcing her to sit still long enough to eat it, reminding her she should refuel her body so she could continue at the same pace. Odd she should remember that about him.

Roland was already seated at one of the round tables draped in a solid white tablecloth when she arrived. The host led her to the table, and he smiled a greeting, looking up from a bowl of lentil soup.

"I hope you don't mind. I ordered an appetizer since you were running late."

Daniella checked the time as she sat down. She was only five minutes late. He must have arrived early and ordered then. Cyrus would have never done that. He would have waited to see what she'd like to eat first.

She ordered water with lemon and smiled at Roland. The dark suit surprised her. At the company he'd helped start up, BoldMine, they seldom wore clothes more formal than khakis and a polo shirt.

He wasn't bad-looking at all. Granted, he didn't have Cyrus's chiseled features, but his close-cropped hair was always short and neat, and he had the most beautiful brown eyes she'd ever seen on a man. Beautiful, but not with the same brooding intensity of Cyrus's.

She silently berated herself. Why couldn't she get him off her mind?

Roland scooted his chair closer to hers. "I have big, important news I want to share with you." He grinned from ear to ear and looked immensely pleased with himself.

"What is it?" Daniella asked.

With a cocky grin, he said, "I'll tell you soon, but we'll need champagne for this."

He piqued her interest with that comment. "Can I get a hint?"

Roland patted her hand. "Patience, my dear. Be patient."

He clearly enjoyed having his little secret, and Daniella didn't want to spoil it. Though she practically knew all the dishes by heart, she perused the menu as they waited for the server to return. She lifted her head when raucous laughter came from the other side of the restaurant. "Someone's having a good time," she murmured.

The comment had been meant for Roland's ears, but the waiter walked up at the same moment with the very recognizable bottle of Armand de Brignac in hand. "There's a group of businessmen in one of our semi-private rooms. They've been here since this afternoon, eating and drinking and spending *a lot* of money."

"Sounds like that will be a nice tip for someone," Daniella commented.

"Yes," the waiter said, a wistful note to his voice. He obviously wished he had been the lucky employee chosen to wait on the group.

They ordered their meals and then the waiter poured them each a glass of champagne.

"I'm getting impatient," Daniella said. "You have to tell me what we're celebrating."

"Success." Roland lifted his glass and she lifted hers. "BoldMine found an investor. We're about to go to the next level." He grinned so widely he could have swallowed his ears.

"You're kidding! I'm so excited for you." She threw an arm around him and gave him a big hug. He'd been working on BoldMine for years, long before they'd met.

He chuckled appreciatively. "Cheers."

They clinked their glasses together and both took substantial swallows of the pricey wine.

"Which means," Roland continued, his voice filled with hidden meaning, "I can help you."

She had no idea what he meant. She wasn't in financial trouble. "Help me how?"

"With your divorce."

Temporarily surprised by the offer, Daniella didn't respond right away. Slowly, she set her glass on the table. "I still don't understand what your success has to do with my divorce."

"I can help financially. With more money you can hire a better attorney to fight and get your divorce. I *want* to help you," Roland said.

"I appreciate your offer, but—"

"Don't brush me off." He set his glass beside hers and leaned forward with an eagerness that made her apprehensive instead of excited. "I'm confident once we sign on the dotted line, the infusion of cash into our software systems will catapult our company, and I will become an extremely wealthy man."

"Maybe or maybe not. You don't know for sure. What if the investor backs out?"

He shook his head, confident. "Everything will be fine," he assured her.

"Even so, I won't accept money from you."

Roland placed a warm hand over hers. "Daniella, you're in this mess because of me. The least I can do is help you get out of it."

"I can't accept your money."

This was her fight, not Roland's. Besides, she was happy with the work Davis performed, although he hadn't been her first choice. Despite their history, she'd wanted a more high profile attorney to handle her divorce. But when she'd left Cyrus, she hadn't moved quickly enough to hire anyone. She'd been preoccupied with settling into her new apartment and resolving problems at work. Cyrus had taken advantage of the delay and "conflicted out" a good number of the top divorce lawyers in the city. By meeting with them and sharing enough details about their marriage to establish an attorney-client relationship, he'd effectively kept them from being able to represent her.

"Yes, you can take money from me. Let me help you so you can become *un*married. Consider it a loan if it'll make you feel better."

Daniella looked at her glass on the table. "As much as I appreciate what you're offering," she said carefully, "I can't let you do that. This is my problem, not yours, and I'll find a way to deal with my husband. Fighting him is not as easy as you think. He has unlimited resources."

"He's not a god, Daniella."

"I know." Not a god, but certainly godlike in the extent of the power and funds available to him.

Roland's jaw hardened. "He's not going to change unless you play hard ball."

"You think I haven't tried?" Daniella asked, frustration lending an edge to her voice. "What makes you think you can defeat him? He has way more money than you or I, and he's not afraid to spend it. You know all about that, don't you?"

An unrecognizable expression flitted across Roland's face. "Yes, I do. So that's it, he's filthy rich and therefore unstoppable. Whereas I'm…what? A pauper compared to him?"

"I wasn't comparing you to him," Daniella said. She placed a hand on his arm, regretting her remark. "He's unstoppable, Roland. He has a team of attorneys and lots of money to spend on them." The conversation was making her lose her appetite.

"*Daniella?*" Her name came as an incredulous query from off to her left. The familiar voice sent the hairs on the back of her neck vertical. She looked up and into the frowning face of her brother-in-law, Trenton Johnson, Cyrus's youngest brother. "What are you doing here?" His green-eyed gaze moved from the bottle of champagne chilling in the bucket to her hand still resting on Roland's arm. His frown deepened.

"I'm having dinner," she said. She left her hand in place in a display of impudence. "What are you doing here?"

"Business dinner," he replied.

Her eyes darted in the general direction of where she'd heard the group of men laughing. Was Cyrus with him? Apprehension skittered down her spine.

Roland cleared his throat, which drew Trenton's attention to him. Roland stood and extended his hand, introducing himself.

Trenton shook the proffered hand. "Trenton Johnson, Daniella's *brother-in-law*." Trenton's emphasis on the relationship was unmistakable and made her feel guilty. But she hadn't done anything wrong. They were simply two friends having dinner.

"Nice to meet you, Trenton," Roland said.

"I'll let you get back to your meal." Trenton was not smiling at all, unusual since he had a gregarious personality, particularly when compared to his oldest sibling. "I'll let Cyrus know I saw you."

Their eyes remained on each other. She could tell he knew she wanted to know if Cyrus was with him.

"Do that," she said with more chutzpah than she felt.

One eyebrow lifted a fraction, but he didn't say anything else before walking away.

"Daniella," Roland said, "he can't hurt you if you don't let him."

Easy for you to say, she thought.

Minutes later, she saw the businessmen leaving, still engaged in a vigorous conversation, laughing as they exited. Trenton was among them, but he didn't turn in her direction, as if he didn't even know she was there. She drained her glass of champagne, her eyes lingering at the end of their short line of bodies. Despite looking forward to the delicious food earlier, she didn't know if she could touch the lamb stew and couscous when they arrived. Her stomach had tangled into a knotted bundle. Would Cyrus make an appearance?

A few more minutes passed and still no Cyrus. A puzzling ache filled her chest, which made no sense, since she didn't actually *want* to see him…did she?

Finally she accepted he wasn't there and relaxed. No doubt Trenton would inform him he'd seen her and Roland together, but at least she didn't have to worry about a confrontation tonight.

She was laughing at one of Roland's comments when, as if he'd been conjured out of thin air, Cyrus came around the corner. Tall and imposing, he weaved his way through the tables filled with diners, an expression on his face that suggested he wanted to hurt someone. All the muscles in her body seized up.

He *had* been here.

She held her breath until his long strides brought him beside their table, a look of displeasure on his face.

He looked down at her without acknowledging Roland with even a glance. "Having fun, Dani?"

CHAPTER SIX

Daniella glared up at her husband in defiance. "Yes, I am."

Roland rose swiftly to his feet. "What a surprise to see you here, Cyrus." A hint of nervousness colored his voice, but he stuck out his hand, reaching across Daniella to do so.

Cyrus's gaze flickered to his outstretched hand, making it clear he saw it, and then dipped back to her. "What do you think you're doing?" He spoke calmly. But didn't he always?

"Eating dinner," she replied in a steady tone.

She didn't want the confrontation to escalate. Beneath Cyrus's deceptively calm exterior lurked a lion ready to pounce at the slightest provocation. He spoke in a low, neutral voice, but his jaw was tight. Even if Roland didn't seem to sense the full extent of the danger, she knew it firsthand. She'd seen Cyrus eviscerate opponents for minor infractions, and considering how much he disliked Roland, she wouldn't be surprised if there was bloodshed.

Their waiter hustled to the table, a ready-to-please expression on his face. "Mr. Johnson, may I get you a chair?"

"That would be nice, thank you. Right here would be fine." He pointed to the spot on Daniella's left, which meant she'd be sandwiched between the two men.

The waiter ran off and almost immediately returned with a chair, which he placed in the exact location Cyrus indicated. The young man never even bothered to ask Roland or her if it was okay to have Cyrus join their table. He assumed it would be, which grated on her nerves.

"The two of you back together now?" Cyrus sat in the chair and rested one shiny black shoe on his knee, patiently waiting for an answer.

She didn't know how to respond. Part of her wanted to thrust a lie in his face and tell him she was romantically involved with Roland, but another part of her worried about the repercussions.

Roland sat down, too, and cleared his throat, no doubt as uncomfortable as she was in this awkward situation.

Cyrus followed up with another question, this time directed at Roland. "You know we're still married, don't you?"

Roland nodded. "I do. But I also know she wants a divorce."

Cyrus's eyes returned to Daniella. He pinned her with a dark stare and she fought the urge to squirm. "She's not getting one. No matter what means she uses to try to get it."

The way he looked at her sent a trickle of nervous energy down her spine. Did he know about the investigator?

"I was going to save this for another time, but since we're all here together, why not do it now? I have to give you credit for trying, by the way." That's when she knew for sure he'd found out about the P.I. and her stomach dropped in dismay. "My driver noticed a dark sedan around more often than not. By the way, your investigator made a good choice, using a nondescript vehicle, but it wasn't good enough. The driver I usually use is former special forces, so he pays attention to details in a way most people don't." He pulled an envelope from his breast pocket, set it on the table, and pushed it toward her. "I received these today and planned to send them to you, but why delay?"

Daniella stared at the envelope, the nervousness in her gut intensifying.

"Go ahead, open it," Cyrus prodded.

Carefully, Daniella opened the envelope and pulled out a stack of photos. Regrettably, the investigator who'd been following Cyrus over the past week could be seen in each one sitting in his car or snapping photos through the long lens of a camera. While he'd been watching them, they'd been watching him.

"Funny thing happened," Cyrus continued, obviously enjoying himself. "We found out who he was working for. I thought he was another low life paparazzi, but imagine my surprise when he mentioned Davis Williams. It was easy enough to figure out this had to do with our divorce, and with a few more questions we found out all the details of your plan. Then I made the problem go away."

Daniella shoved the pictures back in the envelope and dropped it on the table. "You paid him off."

"It's amazing what people will do when you quadruple their fee. Sad, isn't it? The lack of ethics in today's society."

"And you exploit it."

"It's not my fault people can be bought." He looked pointedly at Roland, who shifted uneasily in his chair. "How are things with your little software company?"

His condescension didn't stop Roland's chest from swelling with pride. "We secured an injection of cash thanks to a generous investor. We're on our way to bigger and better things, and our software will change the world."

"Is that right? You made good use of the million dollars I gave you after all. I had my doubts."

"Stop it," Daniella said, embarrassed for Roland.

"It's inventory tracking software, isn't it?" Cyrus asked. Something about the tone of his voice gave Daniella the distinct impression Cyrus already knew the answers to his questions.

"Yes. It'll aid manufacturers and retailers in communicating better than ever. We're about to change Just-In-Time into In-The-Moment."

He sounded proud of his accomplishments, and he should be. He'd worked hard for years to get to this point.

"I'm happy for you, but I thought I told you to stay away from my wife."

"That's enough," Daniella hissed. "Do you have to be so rude?"

"I paid him a million dollars. Despite my wealth, a million dollars is not a little bit of money."

"That was more than four years ago," Roland said.

Cyrus's glaze slid to Roland, his eyes as black and hard as coal. "A deal is a deal, and I don't like it when people renege on deals."

Roland licked his lips. "Give me some time, and I'll give you the money back."

"I don't want the money. I want you to stay away from my wife."

"What I do, when I do it, and with whom, is none of your business," Daniella interjected.

"That's where you're wrong," Cyrus said. "Everything you do is my business because it affects me and reflects on our marriage. Therefore, I forbid you to see this snake again." He spoke in an imperious tone, as if he thought she'd simply fall in line with his dictate.

"Snake? Wait a damn minute," Roland blustered.

"Roland, please." Daniella could feel frustration course through her body. Back and forth, back and forth they went, and she was caught in the middle. She took a deep breath. "Cyrus, you can't forbid me to see anyone, and even though you found out about the investigator, I'm not done. I won't give up."

"You're wasting precious time. Neither of us is getting any younger."

"We should leave," Daniella murmured to Roland. She stood and both men promptly followed suit.

"Time is up, Dani," Cyrus warned.

She looked up into his granite features. "You don't scare me."

His mouth twitched into a half-smile. He seldom smiled, and

more often than not, when he did, he wore that damned half-smile. Which she hated. It reeked of arrogance and a superiority complex—fed by the way people danced around him, rushed to do his bidding, and damn near curtsied in his presence.

He leaned in close again and she stiffened her spine, forcing herself not to withdraw. He whispered in her ear, "There are consequences for your actions. I hope you can live with them."

His scent surrounded her, and a mixture of fear and arousal caused a faint tremor to rattle through her system.

"I can live with them, as long as they get me away from you," she whispered back. His mouth was inches away from hers, and her bottom lip tingled with the inexplicable urge to kiss him.

"Well, I guess I've been told. I should slink away with my tail between my legs, since I've been utterly defeated." The corners of his mouth curved even higher. "Enjoy the rest of your meal."

Before she guessed his intent, Cyrus placed a firm hand at her waist and pulled her into him. The impact with his hard body sent a shockwave of hunger straight to her core. Placing a hand on his arm, she leaned back from him.

"Cyrus." Her voice should have been a firm dismissal. Instead it came out breathless and trembling.

He pressed his mouth to hers and she gasped, taken by surprise. Cyrus didn't make public displays of affection. He'd never held her hand or even given her a peck on the cheek in the presence of others. The most he'd ever done was place a hand at the base of her spine, a comforting gesture meant to show they were together or to guide her in the direction he wanted so he could introduce her to so-and-so from such-and-such a company.

This was not about affection, though. The kiss informed her and Roland of his intentions toward her. It was nothing but a stamp, forcing her to accept to whom she belonged. His mouth pressed hard into hers, and then he swiped the tip of his tongue just inside her lips before lifting his head.

She barely noticed the other customers openly staring at them. Her swamped senses buzzed from the contact. The kiss was so short. It couldn't have lasted more than two seconds, three at the most. Yet every single cell in her body screamed for more.

"How dare you," she said, trying to save face. She lifted a hand to her throbbing mouth.

Cyrus let his hand slide along her waist and down her hip before letting her go. He didn't take his gaze from her, and she saw the moment something shifted and unshakeable resolve entered his eyes. "Time's up," he repeated, his voice rough around the edges.

He walked away and left her standing there, a bit disoriented, a bit confused. He was out of sight before she realized she'd been holding her breath. What alarmed her even more was her own lack of action. Not once had she considered, much less tried, to pull away.

"Are you all right?"

She jumped when Roland touched her arm. She'd forgotten he was there, completely consumed by Cyrus's presence. She could still feel the heat from his hand on the curve of her hip.

"I'm fine," she mumbled.

He'd said her time was up. If she didn't do as he demanded, he would retaliate against her. But how? What could he possibly do?

Now was a waiting game. One where she had to wait to see what the ramifications of her actions would be.

CHAPTER SEVEN

Daniella unlocked the doors to Beaux-Arts Galleries, located along a tree-lined street in downtown Ballard where historic storefronts remained intact. She had managed to carve out a popular showroom that over the past few years had emerged as a coveted venue for both new and established artists.

Walking down the avenue, a visitor easily gained an impression of what the area might have been like back in the late 1800's when it was first settled and filled with lumber mills. The quaint neighborhood contained stylish boutiques, restaurants, coffee shops, and other galleries. Every second Saturday, a Chamber of Commerce-sponsored art walk brought visitors to the neighborhood and provided exceptional foot traffic which had helped her business grow. Beaux-Arts not only sold prints and original paintings to the general public, she and her two salespersons consulted with businesses that wanted to freshen their décor. They also worked with private collectors who viewed art as not only a decoration, but an investment as well.

Her business was couched between a glass-blowing studio on one side and a handmade jewelry store on the other. Across the street, an independent bookstore sat crammed full of books. She liked to go there sometimes on her break and browse the shelves. She'd found a gem once—an old edition of *Invisible Man* by Ralph Ellison. She hadn't been able to resist adding it to her small collection of rare titles. Purchasing it had been a splurge for sure, back when she had money to spend on such things. Nowadays most of her disposable income went toward fighting Cyrus.

The gallery was closed today because she and her staff would be welcoming three groups of underprivileged kids at different times during the day to the gallery to learn more about the world of art and to create their own paintings. It was something they did once a year, but she'd love to do it more often.

All of her employees gladly participated. In addition to the three salespersons, she employed an office manager, a framer, and an in-house portrait painter. If her plans went well, she'd soon have Beaux-Arts Deux, a New York location, which would employ a gallery director, five salespersons, two framers, and an office manager. She had been tweaking her business plan for months but still hadn't approached the bank. New York could make or break her business, and though she hadn't admitted it to anyone, she worried about being able to succeed there.

While she waited for her staff to arrive to help her set up, Daniella looked at the contract from the Manhattan hotel owner who wanted her to provide artwork to complement their new color scheme in the next few months. This was the opportunity she'd been waiting for to expand her business. With this contract in hand, she would be able to go to the bank and show she would have money coming in, which meant she could lease the Manhattan space she'd had her eye on. Last she'd checked, no one had taken over the lease, but it would only be a matter of time. Even in a down market, prime properties there didn't last long.

She sat back in the chair. Why didn't she feel more satisfaction at this accomplishment? There was a time when the idea of having a New York office had made her tingle from head to toe. While getting this contract was a victory for sure, the excitement she expected hadn't manifested. Maybe because she didn't have the space yet.

The front door bell rang, but she ignored it. It wasn't unusual for prints to be delivered on the weekend, but she wasn't expecting any today. When the person at the front leaned on the buzzer for a long time, though, she could no longer ignore the sound and left her office to walk up front.

Roland stood outside. She quickly opened the door to him, taking in the distress on his face. "What's wrong?" she asked.

Lines of strain bracketed his mouth. "I lost my position at BoldMine."

Her eyes widened. "What? You're the chief technology officer. Your work is invaluable, and they need you."

She repeated what he'd told her in the past. He'd been with the start-up company from the beginning, working closely with the two brothers who made up the other chief officers. The injection of cash from their new private investor would help the company enhance the features of its inventory software and increase its business development partnerships with key players in the manufacturing industry. This was the chance he'd been waiting for.

"Apparently, they don't need me," he said bitterly. "The investor purchased a majority stake in our firm, and the next thing I knew, I was removed as CTO. I received my marching papers last night." He thrust a dismissal letter at her.

"Only you?" Daniella took the correspondence, feeling terrible for him. Just a week ago at The Savory Date, she'd warned him about celebrating too soon, but he certainly wouldn't appreciate hearing "I told you so." To be honest, this was worse than anything she'd imagined.

"Just me," Roland confirmed in the same acidic-sounding voice.

Daniella scanned the paper and right away recognized the name of the company that had made the investment.

"Oh no." Her stomach plummeted as nausea buffeted her insides, and she almost dropped the sheet. Even if she hadn't recognized the company name, the bold signature at the bottom would have given her all the information she needed. She couldn't stop staring at the words.

Roland stated the obvious. "Your husband's venture capitalist firm bought a majority stake in our company and had me dismissed."

Her gaze met Roland's. "I'm so sorry."

"I can't see you anymore, Daniella. I'm done." She'd never seen Roland angry, yet from his tone he clearly blamed her for the current turn of events. But *he* had contacted *her*, not the other way around.

"Roland, I swear to you, if I'd known—"

He held up his hand. "Save it. If *I'd* known this would be the result of being seen with you, I would have never gotten involved. I've lost everything. *Everything* I've worked for over the past seven years."

She couldn't imagine the anguish he must be experiencing after expecting to see all his hard work pay off, only to be blindsided by this unexpected disaster. "I'm sorry." She sounded like a broken record, but she didn't know what else to say.

"So am I," he said, his face contorted into a bitter scowl. "I'm going to give Cyrus what he wanted in the first place. I won't be contacting you again, and please don't contact me."

She grabbed the sleeve of his shirt, detaining him. "Wait, there must be something I can do, some way I can help you."

"You really want to help me?" he asked. "Get me my goddamn business back."

Daniella watched as he left. Numb, she clutched the letter in her hand. She had to see Cyrus, and she had to make him stop.

****

Cyrus lived northwest of downtown in one of the most popular neighborhoods in the Seattle area and had bought his house before he married Daniella. The location suited him, being close to the city for a quick commute, and its location on a hill was conducive to his weekend exercise regimen. On any given Saturday he could be found jogging the tree-lined streets past the historic homes that dotted the landscape. He ran in peace here. In this affluent area, his neighbors barely registered his presence, for which he was grateful.

He hadn't exercised today because he'd recently arrived home after a short business trip to Las Vegas. He was tired as hell, but nothing could have kept him from his niece's ninth birthday party. He came straight from the airport, still dressed in the suit he'd donned earlier for the weekend meeting with a hotelier who owned several casinos. They were interested in making Full Moon beer the exclusive brand they carried, with the possibility to expand around the country. Cyrus was pretty sure he'd sealed the deal and expected a follow up within a few weeks, at which time he'd bring in his brother, Trenton, to cover the marketing side of the arrangement.

Cyrus parked his car in the garage and dropped his bags at the foot of the stairs. Without prompting, one of the servants appeared and took the bags up to his bedroom.

Gift in hand, he headed to the pool house. His niece, Katie, had wanted a pool party, and initially Ivy—his only sister—had planned to have it at the Four Seasons Hotel where they lived. Then she'd changed her mind and asked him if she could have it at his place instead, to which he'd readily agreed.

He was crazy about his niece and hoped one day to fill his house with children as energetic and intelligent as she was. Her birth had brought so much happiness to the family, particularly since she'd arrived only months after his father died. In some ways, she had saved their family, shaking them out of the deep-rooted sadness at having lost their father so unexpectedly.

At the pool house he encountered a bunch of 8 and 9-year-old girls running and splashing in the water. Besides Ivy, two other mothers kept an eye on the screaming prepubescents. As he approached, one of the girls stood poised on the diving board and did a graceful dive into the water, receiving a series of enthusiastic cheers and claps from her friends.

Music from the latest pop sensation blared from the external speakers. Hired help was on hand to assist with the food prep and serving, and when the girls grew tired and wanted to relax, the pool house contained plenty of seating and an entertainment center to keep them busy for hours with music, videos, and games.

Cyrus took a seat, and before he announced his presence, Katie saw him.

"Uncle Cyrus!" she screamed. She separated from her group of friends and scampered over, dripping wet, her long braids weighted down with water and trailing behind her.

"Katie, you'll get him wet," Ivy cautioned, waving her hands in an effort to stop her, but Katie was undeterred. She flung her arms around his neck, soaking his jacket with pool water.

Ivy came over, a chastising frown on her face.

"It's okay," Cyrus told his sister. He squeezed Katie with one arm around her tiny waist. "Happy birthday," he murmured.

She pulled back and grinned. "Thank you." Unable to contain her excitement, she hopped from one foot to the next, eyeing the wrapped box in his hand. She already knew what he'd brought. Last year, he'd promised to get it for her. "Is that for me?"

"Is there another birthday girl here?" he teased.

She giggled and shook her head vigorously. Droplets of water from her hair dripped onto his handmade leather shoes. "I'm the only one."

"Then I guess it's yours."

She snatched the box and turned to Ivy. "Can I open it now? I don't want to wait to open it with my other presents."

"Yes, you may."

The words had barely left her mother's mouth before Katie tore into the colored paper and torn fragments were floating to the ground.

She opened the box and pulled out the gold-plated cell phone that lay inside. Her eyes widened to double their normal size. Because purple was her favorite color, he'd had amethysts added around the frame as a surprise.

Holding up the phone so her mother could see, she squealed, "Mommy, look!"

"I see," Ivy said dryly. Now she directed her disapproval at Cyrus.

Katie flung her arms around him again and kissed his cheek. He held onto her tiny body just as tight. She smelled like chlorine and the sweetness of little girls her age. "Thank you so much. I love you, Uncle Cyrus."

He kissed her temple. "Love you, too, Munchkin."

She grinned and ran toward her friends to show off her gift.

"Don't get it wet," Ivy called after her.

"It's water proof," Cyrus said.

"Of course it is." Ivy placed both hands on her hips. "I try to keep her grounded and you do your best to spoil her."

He shrugged. "What are you worried about? You're doing a fine job. She's a great kid."

"Well, still..." Ivy demurred, obviously pleased by the comment. "Did you have to buy her something so extravagant?"

"That's what uncles do. Besides, Mother and Father gave us extravagant gifts, and we turned out fine."

"*We* did?" She arched an eyebrow and a faint smile came to her lips. "You're spoiled."

"I like nice things. That's not the same as being spoiled." Cyrus rose to his feet. Their father used to tell them they should never let anyone make them feel ashamed for enjoying the fruits of their labor, and he wholeheartedly agreed. He worked hard, and he should be allowed to indulge in the luxuries that came with their level of wealth.

Knowing it was a waste of time to argue with him, Ivy pursed her lips. "Thank you. I know how much you love her and she adores you."

She came closer and studied him. "You okay? You look tired."

"I am tired," he admitted, rolling his neck. "But I have more work to do before I can take a break."

"When was the last time you had a vacation? You can't keep up this pace."

"Says who?"

She sighed wearily, as if talking to an obstinate child. "You need to take care of yourself. You're not indestructible. Remember what happened before."

Of all his siblings, Ivy was definitely the biggest worrier. Perhaps it was the nurturing part of her personality, but she always wanted to make sure everyone else was doing okay. It had been years since the incident she referenced, but Ivy was prone to bringing it up. During a short period in his life, he'd become vulnerable, and he'd much prefer to forget it and never go through the experience again.

"I'm fine. I eat right and I exercise."

"Rest has to be part of the equation, too."

"I'll rest when I'm dead," he said, to which she frowned. He changed the subject. The conversation about working too hard had been belabored to death. "Did Trenton stop by?"

"He did and gave Katie her gift."

"So he actually made time."

"I think he realized he didn't have a choice after the tongue-lashing you gave him when he said he didn't have time to attend a child's birthday party. And just so you know, Xavier called and wished her a happy birthday." Xavier was the second oldest.

"Glad to know he took a minute from saving the world to make his niece happy. What about your twin?"

Ivy's eyes clouded over. "We didn't hear from him."

That response displeased Cyrus. Gavin could have spared a few minutes to call his niece. Cyrus had also been annoyed when Ivy told him Gavin didn't know if he could make it to her engagement party.

Whatever Gavin was doing was not nearly as important as making sure Katie experienced all the attention she deserved on her special day or making Ivy happy on hers.

"Finally, another man," a relieved male voice said behind him. Cyrus turned to see Lucas, his sister's fiancé and Katie's father, coming toward them with a grocery sack in his hand. "I was hoping when I came back from the store there'd be another man here. Tell me you're staying."

Lucas lived in Atlanta, but he visited Seattle often. At first, Cyrus hadn't cared for him, suspecting he could be one of the many users who came into their lives, but he'd turned out to not be so bad after all. Not only had he been good for Ivy, his relationship with Katie had grown strong. Based on his treatment of them, he'd earned Cyrus's respect, and he had to give the man credit for keeping such a good attitude despite the initial opposition from Cyrus to having him in their lives.

"I came to give Katie her birthday gift," Cyrus replied. "I've got work to do, so you're on your own."

"You're stuck with us females," Ivy said to Lucas, looking at him with love in her eyes.

Cyrus took this as his cue to depart. He said goodbye and waved at his niece.

On his way inside, he turned back to tell Ivy to save him a piece of cake, and caught her and Lucas in a kiss. He lingered, observing the affection between them. When they withdrew, Lucas whispered something to her and Ivy laughed. Lucas then pulled her close again, this time for a kiss to the forehead.

Cyrus turned away from the sight. He and Daniella had been like them once—or at least close to it. Until she'd grown tired of him. He rubbed away the sharp prick of pain that jabbed his chest.

It was his fault his marriage had broken down. His fault spirited debates over politics and religion were no longer shared over breakfast.

His fault he could no longer sit beside her at business dinners and listen, proudly, as she held her own against captains of industry. Intelligent, articulate, and beautiful. The type of woman any man would be proud to call his own. His fault he could no longer wake up next to her or feel her warm body curl into his, seeking warmth in his arms.

But he would change the situation. Soon.

In his office, he pulled off his jacket and placed the damp garment on the wooden coat tree in the corner. He dropped into the chair behind his desk, picked up his tension ball and squeezed it rapidly in succession.

He had to get her back. Closing his eyes, he rested his head against the back of the chair and squeezed the sphere of rubber even tighter.

Sighing heavily, he set down the ball. He couldn't dwell on his relationship with Daniella all day. He dialed the number for his personal assistant, Shaun.

"I need you to take care of something for me. This takes priority over anything else."

"Okay," Shaun replied.

"Call my brother Gavin and have him call me back," he said. "If you don't get him when you call, try every half hour for the next four hours." Gavin might find it easy to ignore Ivy's requests, but Cyrus knew exactly how to get his attention. "After that, you can have the rest of the night off."

He hung up the phone and went to work.

Chapter Eight

Daniella pulled up to the gate of the house she'd shared with Cyrus for a year and sat there, waiting. It was nightfall and the neighborhood was quiet.

As luck would have it, the gates swung inward to let out a vehicle. It was the van from Aldi's Market; they'd probably dropped off Cyrus's weekly grocery delivery. No change there—everything on schedule. She gripped the steering wheel and slipped in on the right side as they drove out on the left. If no one was paying close attention to the video camera trained at the gate's entrance, she'd have the element of surprise on her side.

She entered the house as if she belonged there and was immediately accosted by the memories. She and Cyrus used to eat breakfast in the kitchen down the hall when he came back from his morning run through the neighborhood. She also recalled reheating meals for a late night dinner and going up to the rooftop patio to enjoy them together under the stars.

Those moments had been special but she couldn't afford to dwell on them now. Nostalgia led the way to weakness.

Now to find him.

She'd only walked a few feet when Ms. Ernestine appeared, her gray and white uniform crisp and clean. Damn.

Officially Cyrus's housekeeper, she also cooked many of his meals and worked closely with the house manager to maintain the house and grounds. Ms. Ernestine eyed her with a surprised smile. They hadn't seen each other since she left. "Mrs. Johnson, what are you doing here?"

"I, um…"

"You're too late for Katie's birthday party," Ms. Ernestine supplied. "The last of them left about thirty minutes ago."

"Oh no, too bad." She tried to gauge the older woman's disposition. Apparently, Cyrus hadn't told her anything negative. "Is Cyrus around? I'd like to talk to him."

Ms. Ernestine stood in place, but her expression remained pleasant. "Mr. Johnson is in his office, working."

Good, she could get him alone right away. Relieved, Daniella smiled. "Thank you."

"It's good to see you again, Mrs. Johnson."

Ms. Ernestine continued on to her destination and Daniella breathed a quiet sigh of relief she'd gotten this far. Nothing at all like the fiasco at the Johnson Enterprises building.

Cyrus's office was at the back of the house where he could work in peace and quiet, so she had quite a walk and plenty of opportunity to see reminders of their life together. Her chest constricted when she saw all of the changes she'd made were still in place. Several contemporary pieces of art lined the walls, and she'd removed the drapes from the windows in the main corridor that ran along one side of the house, leaving them bare to allow in plenty of light.

Her steps slowed at the entrance to the reading room. Books lined the shelves and a skylight allowed sunshine to pour in without restriction. The Chinese powder-blue vase she'd set on one of the bookshelves remained in place. Cyrus hadn't been fond of the color, and she'd fully expected it to be gone.

Why *had* he left it there? Why had he left any of it—the paintings, the wall hangings, even furniture remained that she'd chosen. How could he live here with all of these reminders of her and their failed marriage?

Because in his eyes, their marriage hadn't failed.

Her confusion gave way to the anger that had prompted this visit. He hadn't removed anything because he'd had every intention of forcing her to come back. By any means necessary.

With her anger freshly nourished by thoughts of Cyrus's manipulative tactics, Daniella started once again toward her destination.

At the end of the quiet corridor, she flung open the door and slammed it behind her, happy to have the element of surprise on her side. Cyrus paused in the middle of pacing behind his desk, tension ball in hand.

For a fleeting second her heart tripped. This was the third time she'd seen him within a short period, and the additional contact was doing strange things to her nerves. So was the fact he didn't have on a suit jacket and looked particularly stylish and attractive wearing a pair of wide suspenders over his white shirt. Tiny vibrations filled her stomach. He'd always looked so damn good in his suspenders— downright delicious, in fact—and this time was no different.

Damn him.

"We need to talk. *Now*," she said. She marched forward and slammed down the correspondence Roland had dropped off. "What is this?"

Cyrus carefully set the ball on the desk and bent over the phone. "Gentlemen, we'll have to postpone this conversation."

Her cheeks flushed hot, and she allowed herself a brief moment of contrition. She hadn't known he was in the middle of a meeting when she barged in.

"I have a hysterical woman in my office and this may take some time to resolve. On Monday I'll have my secretary contact you to reschedule our meeting." He hit a button and turned off the speaker.

Daniella bristled at the disparaging remark he used to describe her. She'd show him hysterical if that's what he really wanted.

"What is this?" She jabbed a finger at the wrinkled letter she'd dropped on his desk.

He slid it toward him and scanned the contents. "Looks like a dismissal letter," he said.

"*Your* dismissal letter. You bought a majority interest in BoldMine, Inc. and fired Roland. How could you? He's worked hard for years to get this company launched."

Cyrus folded his arms across his chest, the movement bringing attention to his hard pecs. Was his chest bigger? Even his biceps looked larger.

"He did such a good job of selling the company at dinner the other night, I have no doubt I made the right decision to invest in BoldMine."

"All of a sudden you're interested in inventory software?" Daniella demanded. His personal investments tended toward real estate and businesses that complemented his family's businesses.

"You know I have a diverse portfolio."

"It's not that damn diverse. Don't patronize me, Cyrus. Your investment had nothing to do with diversifying your portfolio. You wanted to destroy his life."

He sat down and rested his hands on the cushioned arms of the chair. Leaning back, his expression turned indolent, uncaring. "Destroy his life? You're being a bit melodramatic, aren't you?"

"If anyone's being dramatic, it's you. Those were your words three years ago, remember? And you followed through. For no good reason, you had Roland dismissed from a company he founded."

"Maybe he should have stayed away from you." His tone grated on her nerves.

That was why no man within the entire city of Seattle would come near her or risk being seen with her. Not while she was still Cyrus Johnson's wife. His power and influence was far reaching.

The Seattle social circle for the rich and famous was small, and every other single man her age—even those who were older—steered clear because of her ties to Cyrus. None of them wanted to risk his wrath—yet another reason she needed to be free of him.

As long as she remained his wife, she couldn't get a date even if she paid for one. She'd dropped the Johnson part of her name after they separated, yet every article about her gallery described her as "the estranged wife of Cyrus Johnson, billionaire brewer and head of Johnson Enterprises." As if the modifying phrase was a title attached to her name. She was inextricably tied to him, with no identity of her own.

"I can't respect a man who goes back on his promise. What choice did I have?" He tried to look apologetic but failed miserably. She wasn't even sure he was really trying. "What were you doing with him anyway?"

"I forgave him for what he did. Who knows, we may rekindle or relationship after you and I divorce."

The comment had been meant to provoke him, but Cyrus chuckled knowingly. He didn't believe a word she said. "You expect me to believe you're going back to him? After being with me? Come on, Dani."

She gritted her teeth at his egotism. "Why didn't you take your revenge out on *me*?" Daniella leaned over the desk. "You had no right to hurt him. This is between you and me."

"I disagree," Cyrus said coolly. "I think any man who knowingly goes out with another man's wife is being damned disrespectful. Not to mention Roland reneged on our original agreement."

"One that was dishonest and deceitful," she reminded.

"One that served his purpose at the time. He took the money."

"He has nothing now."

"That's not my problem." His jaw hardened. "All things considered, you should thank me for the mercy I showed him," he said in a vicious undertone.

"If you think destroying a man's livelihood and everything he's ever worked for is being merciful, you have a warped sense of what exactly mercy is."

"I took his business, but I could have done much worse. I could have destroyed him and everything he knows. No one comes between me and what's mine." His face had darkened into possessive anger. "Now he knows better."

"I'm *not* yours."

"You are mine. You see this?" He showed her the back of his hand, bringing attention to his platinum wedding ring. "I take my vows seriously. You're mine, and I'm yours. You don't get to walk away on a whim."

Daniella took a good look at her husband—the stubborn set of his jaw, the way his eyes met hers in challenge. More than ever, it became clear she fought a losing battle. The draining power of defeat seeped into her limbs.

"You're never going to stop, are you?" she asked quietly.

"You're my wife, Dani. It's time that you come home."

She took a deep breath, loathe to give in, but the never-ending fight with him was taking a toll on her bank account and her sanity.

Time to end the standoff.

Bracing herself, she looked her husband squarely in the eyes. "Okay."

He stilled. "Okay what?"

"I'll do my best to give you a child."

For the first time ever, Daniella saw Cyrus speechless. He clearly couldn't believe she had caved even though he'd done everything in his power to ensure she did. His eyes probed her face, searching for any sign of trickery.

"Do you understand what that means?" he asked.

She nodded. "I do. After I...have the baby, you'll give me a divorce?"

His face remained expressionless. "Yes."

Daniella nodded her acceptance of his terms and took out her smartphone. She tapped the calendar app and launched into a matter-of-fact conversation about the particulars.

"The best chance for fertilization is when I'm ovulating, of course," she said in an unemotional voice. She had to disassociate herself from the idea or she'd never go through with it. "We can both keep track of the dates and times. My next menstrual cycle is—"

"What the hell are you talking about?" Cyrus came to his feet and stared across the desk at her as if she'd lost her mind. His eyebrows dipped over his eyes. "*Fertilization?*" He said the word as if he'd never heard it before.

"Yes," Daniella said with a tight smile. "That's what the sperm does to the egg so a child can grow inside of me. Surely they taught you all about it in the expensive private school your parents paid for you to attend...?"

"I know what fertilization is," Cyrus said slowly, wrestling with impatience. "But that's not exactly the word I would use to describe what we're about to do."

Daniella shrugged one shoulder. "Fine, procreation. Better? It really doesn't matter what we call it. We're making a baby." She bent her head to her calendar again. "I'll talk to my doctor about the options available for us to reproduce."

"The options available—" Cyrus ran his hand down the back of his head, as if he couldn't even let himself finish repeating the words. Pinching his nose, he closed his eyes, and when he opened them again, she didn't like the determined look in them. "There seems to be some kind of misunderstanding." He spoke in a deliberate, slow voice. The tone disturbed her and sent a frisson of unease down her spine "You're my wife. We're having a child."

"I understand that, and we need to know what options are available to us to do this."

He laughed then, a heavy, deep chuckle that brightened his features. It was a real laugh this time, and she hadn't seen him in the throes of true humor in so long she could only stare. The carved lines of his face softened and stirred something in her chest. Feelings she'd long ago discarded because they threatened her objectivity.

He put his hand to his stomach. "I haven't laughed that hard in a long time." He came around the desk with a slow gait. "There's only one option available for us to 'do this.'"

Her mind shied away from the direction she suspected he was going in. "There are several options," she insisted. "There's IVF, GIFT..." She trailed off when he shook his head, dismissing her suggestions.

"We're not having fertility problems."

"That doesn't mean we can't use those options."

"Actually, it does. Because I have absolutely no intention of getting doctors, tubes, or petri dishes involved." He stopped in front of her, no further away than an outstretched arm could reach. "We're going to have sex."

That word—sex—conjured images of naked flesh and sweat slick bodies. She felt cornered, even though plenty of room existed in the large office.

Suddenly tongue-tied, Daniella fumbled for the right words. She'd had no idea of the extent of his expectations. "We don't have to...have sex...there are options..." Her voice faltered.

"The only options are the ones I'm about to give you," he said. "You're going to move back into our home and wear your rings." He came closer and whispered the next words. "And you're going to spend every night in our bed."

CHAPTER NINE

He was staring at her mouth, and Daniella felt the beginning pulse of a dangerous heat on the inside of her thighs. She shook her head forcefully at the dizzying effect of their conversation. She was having a lot of trouble with three letter words today. First *sex*, now *bed*. His warm tone and the images it conjured made her body throb in a very particular, suddenly damp spot—as if he'd licked her there.

"You're out of your mind," she said. "That is not going to happen. Isn't it enough I agreed to your ridiculous request? Now you want to…"

"There's chemistry between us. Always has been from the beginning. That hasn't changed."

"Maybe on your end."

He captured her gaze, eyeing her with skepticism. "Are you saying you're no longer attracted to me? That I can no longer make your toes curl?"

Inside her patent leather heels, her toes contracted. "That's exactly what I'm saying."

A slow smile spread across his full lips. The type of smile a fox had right before it raided the hen house. "Prove it."

Her breathing arrested for a nanosecond, but she quickly

recovered. "How am I supposed to do that?"

"Kiss me."

"We kissed at The Savory Date."

"That was a peck on the lips. I want you to give me a real kiss, and if you don't feel anything, then we do it your way."

"No." She backed up a couple of feet. It was a trap, one that would ensnare her for sure. "I don't have to prove anything to you."

"Scared?" The softly spoken word was filled with mocking challenge.

"I told you before I'm not afraid of you." She lifted her chin with a boldness she was far from feeling.

"Then give me a kiss." He ate the distance between them with one long stride. "One little kiss, and if you prove me wrong, we do this your way."

She lowered her lids against the seductive quality of his voice and stared down at the rich burgundy carpet. Her breathing had already grown fractured at the mere thought of kissing him.

"You know this color lipstick is my favorite," he said. His fingertip swept the seam of her lips and made them tingle. "It's distracting. Is that why you wore it? So you could distract me?"

She'd forgotten she was wearing ruby red lipstick. In truth he preferred her to be au naturale, but when she wasn't his favorite color lipstick was ruby red. He said the color gave her lips a fullness and plumpness which turned her mouth into an invitation, begging to be kissed.

"I didn't wear it for you," she said.

He took her hand, and a shiver of awareness raced up her arm. He ran the blunt tip of his thumb over the spot where her rings used to be. Her pulse started to dance, faster and faster. "One little kiss, Dani." He pressed his lips to the back of her fingers.

The inside of her belly trembled, as if a family of moths had taken up residence there. He pulled her closer, and she went to him with little resistance. She was shaking. She wanted him to kiss her. Badly.

One hand went to her back and trailed up and down her spine in a slow caress. Despite his cold, cruel nature in business, Cyrus was a sensual man and a master of seduction.

He drew her closer until she pressed against him. He was semi-erect, fitting because she was semi-wet.

Against the stimulus of his hard chest, her nipples pebbled and her breathing became shallow. She felt his hard strength and fought the reaction the best she could, not wanting to give him the satisfaction of being right.

His labored breathing could be heard in the quiet room. "Do you know how long it's been since you left me?" he asked. "Three years, one month, eighteen days."

Her heart pounded, echoing in her ears. He'd kept track, even down to the day?

"And five hours," he added.

Her lips parted in shock.

"I know exactly how long you've been gone, and it's been even longer since we've made love," he said. "One little kiss, Dani." His breath brushed her mouth and created a tingling sensation across the skin of her lips. "One little kiss for your husband."

It wouldn't be one little kiss. She knew it and was certain he did, too. He would consume her, because that's what he did. She lost all sense of the present and time when caught up in his arms.

Cyrus lowered his head, and in the next instant their lips fused together. This kiss was different from the one at the restaurant. It was tender, even affectionate, and Daniella leaned in, enjoying the flavor of him way too much. She held onto his biceps, the power and strength of his arms sending little darts of pleasure along her spine.

Engulfed in the thrill of touching him again, she was unable to move away, and she certainly didn't want to. His lips were warm, and little by little he increased the pressure against hers. The hand at her back dipped to her backside and tightened. She gasped into his mouth, the blossom of heat invading her thighs.

When he lifted his head, she felt bereft, and he must have felt it too, because his nostrils flared and he groaned—the sound in the back of his throat so low she almost didn't hear it. Need flashed in his half-closed eyes. He dipped his head again and heaven help her, she lifted her mouth to meet his and parted her lips for his invasion.

A few seconds before there had been no tongue, just their lips meeting, reacquainting with each other. This time, his tongue foraged into her mouth and the arm around her waist tightened, drawing her even closer against the swelling hardness of him.

"Damn, I love kissing you," he muttered. He wasn't only concerned about his own needs. He wanted to make sure she enjoyed it, too. He was amazingly thorough, and oh-so-good at it. Just like he was at everything else.

Her muscles became useless, as if they'd atrophied. She didn't move, simply melted against him and enjoyed the way he took control, tilting her head back, devouring her, claiming her again.

Her arms inched around his neck and she opened even more to him. She traced the shape of his mouth with her tongue and felt the violent tremor that rocked his hard frame. Hands at the back of her thighs, he lifted her onto the desk. Shoving items out of the way, he cleared a space and lowered her onto her back, and she welcomed his heavy bulk between her open legs.

Burning up, Cyrus fumbled with the buttons on her silk blouse, careful even though he wanted to yank the edges apart and tear it off of her. He finally peeled back the material to reveal a black, lacy number that barely covered her soft skin. He popped the front clasp and her sweet breasts bounced free, forcing her to emit a slight whimper. Plump, with engorged nipples standing upright like little caramel party hats, they called to his mouth. He lowered his head and before he even touched them, she was arching her back and gripping his head, anticipating his touch.

He didn't want to hurt her, but he could barely contain himself. He'd been deprived for so long, he devoured her breasts, having suffered without the taste of her for what seemed like eons.

Control. Rigid control. That's how he'd kept it together the past few years. But now that she was lying beneath him and he could feel the heat between her legs, he couldn't fathom how he'd managed for so long without storming her apartment and dragging her back here.

"Dani…"

He wet her nipple with the pull of his lips, swiping his teeth over the puckered flesh and then following up with soothing strokes of his tongue. His ears ate up every moan, every broken plea of her surrender. Sounds that could turn even the most impotent man into a Casanova.

He ran his hand down the middle of her chest and massaged her breasts, squeezing them and alternating by deliberately rubbing the dark flesh of her nipples between his finger and thumb. Each time he did she let loose a little moan and her face contorted into a pained expression.

Through his pants Cyrus could feel how hot she was. He reached between them to undo his belt, his only thought to ease the pain of the southward rush of blood. He'd already undone the buckle when he hesitated, registering during a moment of lucidity this was neither the time nor the place. When he and Dani made love again, he wanted to go slow and savor every inch of her. He wanted to bury his head between her legs and inhale her musky, feminine perfume and lick at her essence with his tongue. This rushed coupling that threatened to overwhelm them would not do.

Her ruby red lips were full and swollen, and he dived back in, kissing her hard, savagely, and taking as much as he could until he could have her beneath him in the proper setting. Her legs came up around his waist and she grinded her hips into his. The sensual motion almost wiped out his resolve, but he lifted his head from the temptation she presented and cupped her cheeks in his hands. Her eyelids fluttered open, and as he looked down at her, the dazed expression in her eyes slowly disappeared and her legs fell away.

"As much as I want to make love to you right now, I know you're not ready," he whispered. It was too soon, and she would regret it. Gently, he pulled her into a sitting position and noted the widening of her eyes. "You're surprised."

"I am." Her voice still held the breathless huskiness of arousal.

She turned away from him, and he could see her embarrassment at her easy capitulation, but as far as he was concerned, that was the way it should be. They'd both been caught up in a tidal wave of desire and emotion.

"You have nothing to be ashamed of," he whispered. "You're my wife, and it's my job to make you feel good, but I don't want us to rush."

"You have surprising restraint." She closed her bra, squeezing her ample bosom to do so and creating the most beautiful cleavage he'd ever seen. His penis jumped. He watched with regret as she started buttoning her blouse and couldn't help but wonder if he'd made the right decision to wait.

He stepped back so she could step down onto the floor. "Not always. Look at my desk," he said. "Look at all the chaos you've caused again." The words had a double meaning. He was talking about something bigger, grander than the desk. He couldn't keep order in his life when Daniella was around.

She kept her head bent, continuing to button the blouse. Her fingers shook a little with each movement. "This didn't exactly go as I'd planned. I guess you were right about us having chemistry."

"You had doubts?" he asked.

"No," she admitted. She finished buttoning her blouse and looked up at him with resignation in her eyes.

He ran a finger down the velvet soft skin of her jawline. She didn't turn away but lowered her lashes. "Ivy's engagement party is next weekend, and I want you to come with me."

Her eyes narrowed a little, and he saw the distrust in the copper-brown depths as clearly as if she'd spoken it out loud. "If we're getting back together, we have to let people know. Why are you making this hard?"

"First of all, we're not getting back together, and you know why I'm being difficult."

"Because you think I can't be trusted."

"You can't. The things you do...to people...it's not right, Cyrus. You can't force everyone to bend to your will every time you get an idea."

Her words disturbed him, but his tactics were the most efficient way he knew to get things done. "It works."

"You can catch more flies with honey, Cyrus. Your way is not the only way."

He didn't say anything at first, merely looked at her, examining her features. "It's not," he conceded.

She seemed surprised he'd agreed with her. "Do you think...will you give Roland his job back?" she asked in a tentative voice.

He watched her closely, trying to gauge if there was more than a friendship between her and Roland. "What does it matter to you?"

"I think it's the right thing to do."

He would make this one concession, but only because she asked. "I don't know why you care about that lowlife, but I'll give him his job back on one condition. He stays the hell away from you. For good this time."

"I'll tell him." He frowned, and she added hastily, "I'll only talk to him to tell him what's going to happen." She tucked her shirt back into her pants and smoothed her hands over hips. "One more thing," she said. She hesitated before she continued, a sign he wouldn't like the next words. "After three months, if I don't get pregnant, you'll give me a divorce."

"No way."

"We can't do this indefinitely. We don't know what will happen. What if we can't get pregnant? You have to give me an out."

Normally Cyrus didn't negotiate if he had the upper hand, content to smash the other party with a take-it-or-leave-it attitude. In this case that behavior wouldn't be necessary.

"Six months," he countered. "Not a day less."

She let out a deep breath and nodded her agreement to the compromise. "Do I have your word?"

"I've never lied to you, Dani. You have my word," he said. "I expect you to move in right away. I'll give you the number to my assistant. He'll help you." He'd have Shaun move her in quickly, before she had a chance to rethink her decision.

"Fine." Daniella walked toward the door.

"And Dani?"

She turned around to face him. "Stay away from Roland DuBois. Let that phone call be the end of your contact with him."

She opened her mouth as if to respond and then changed her mind. She walked out of his office, and after the door closed, Cyrus reclaimed his chair and looked at the disorder of his desk. He ran his hand over his hair and closed his eyes to relive the past few moments.

He *had* to get her back. He was in love with her. The realization had sneaked up on him unexpectedly three years ago when she left. The gut-wrenching pain he'd experienced when she'd walked away had been almost unbearable, but he'd thrown himself into work to get through it.

Once she came back, they could start over. She was the only woman he wanted, the only one he could imagine spending the rest of his life with, and the only one he wanted to be the mother of his children.

No matter how much acrimony existed between them, he didn't want Daniella back for six months, for a year, not for any limited period of time.

As far as he was concerned, she was coming back for good.

CHAPTER TEN

"Thank you. It was a pleasure doing business with you."

Daniella shook hands with the president and vice president of the software company she'd spent the last hour reviewing prints with. Today she was in Bellevue. The suburb had seen major growth in recent years as more and more start-ups and small businesses set up shop in the Seattle area. The city was emerging as a rival of Silicon Valley as tech companies took advantage of the affordable office space and attractive tax incentives.

The meeting had been successful. The company had recently leased office space in Bellevue and wanted the decor to reflect their young staff and the president's love of music. She'd taken several catalogues, as well as some prints by local artists whose work she thought was a good fit. The president had liked one of the artists so much, they'd discussed framed originals for his own home. Once in the car, she called one of her salespersons, gave her the details, and instructed her to get in touch with the artist's agent to get the ball rolling on brokering a deal.

Driving across the bridge that spanned Lake Washington, she was on her way back to Seattle. While she should be excited about the pending deal, tonight would not only be her first night back at home with Cyrus, they would attend his sister's engagement party as a couple. Apprehension settled in her stomach and wouldn't go away.

Packing up her belongings and moving them into the mansion hadn't taken long at all with Shaun taking care of the details. He'd promised to have her unpacked by tonight, and she didn't doubt he could do it.

She drove to Viva on Broadway Avenue, a popular coffee shop many Seattleites considered had the best coffee in Seattle. She didn't pay much attention to the few patrons at the tables before walking up to the curved bar and placing an order for two one-pound bags of her favorite blend.

On her way back out the door she paused at the familiar stride of a man coming toward her wearing a golf shirt and tan slacks. At the sight of her father, Daniella's lungs ceased to function. She hadn't seen him in so long, she temporarily froze. Tall and handsome, with a dark bronze complexion—partly compliments of a Spanish mother and black father, and partly from being exposed to the sun's rays year round at his home in Miami—he turned heads though well into his sixties.

Pretending not to see him, Daniella ducked her head and hurried to the door, but he'd seen her. "Daniella!"

She didn't want to speak to him, but there was no way she could behave as if she hadn't heard him call her name. Taking a deep breath, she swung around and transformed her face into an uninterested mask.

"Carlos." A long time ago she'd started calling him by his first name. He didn't deserve the title of father.

Despite her unenthusiastic greeting, he looked happy to see her, his brown eyes bright and eager. He looked her up and down, smiling as if they had a good relationship. "What a surprise," he said. "It's good to see you. I didn't think I'd be able to see you while I was back in town."

"If you wanted to make sure you saw me, you could have called and set up a meeting," she said a cool voice.

"Would you have met with me?" he asked, his voice hopeful.

"No, I wouldn't have," she said with a tight smile, and was satisfied when she saw the smile waver on his lips.

"Of course not."

"Did you want something?"

"Yes, I..." He rubbed the back of his neck. "Do you think we could sit and talk for a few minutes?"

"About what?"

"I have something to tell you."

She glanced at the clock hanging on the wall behind the cash register. "I only have a few minutes," she said, even though she had no other pressing appointment.

He nodded his understanding. "I only need a few minutes." He glanced around the shop and motioned with his hand. "How about we sit over there?"

Sit down and talk to her father. She couldn't remember the last time that happened, and all of a sudden she was frightened of the situation she was placing herself in. But why should she be fearful? He couldn't hurt her anymore.

"A few minutes," she repeated.

"No problem."

He led the way to a two-top table against the window. Located at the back, it lent an air of privacy.

Daniella set her purse and coffee purchase on the table. What could her father possibly have to say to her after all this time?

"You look so much like your mother," he said softly.

She stiffened. Wrong start to the conversation, and he realized it right away, too.

"I'm sorry, I shouldn't have—"

"No, you shouldn't have. What do you want?"

He took a deep breath. "I came back here to close on the house," he said.

Daniella shrugged. "I figured as much."

The house he referred to was the property he'd purchased years ago when he and her mother first married. He'd allowed her and Daniella to live there after their divorce, but his name remained on the deed. After her mother passed away, he rented the property to long term tenants who'd moved out over a year ago. It had take over a year on the market before the property finally sold.

Her mother had lived there until her death from colon cancer. The disease had metastasized, spreading throughout the tissues of her body at an alarming rate. The chemotherapy treatments left her so weak she could no longer work, could barely even walk most days. Even with the aggressive treatments, the cancer had plowed through her cells and ravaged her body until she'd been so withered she was unrecognizable, only a fragment of former self.

"The reason I'm glad we were able to see each other today is because I have something to tell you." He rubbed his hands together, apparently finding it difficult to tell her his news. She wished he'd get it over with. "I'm leaving the country. I'm selling the house in Miami, too, and moving to the Caribbean at the end of the year."

Moving? For good? The shock of his words left her temporarily speechless. Daniella swallowed. "I see."

"I was hoping—"

"Don't you mean we?" she interrupted him. Hurt, anger foamed inside of her. "You said 'I'm leaving the country,' but what you really mean is *we're* leaving the country. You and your wife. Are your sons going, too?"

"No, the boys aren't going. Just me and…my wife." He leaned across the table. "Before I go, I want…I wanted to see if we could patch things up. I want you to have my address, in case you ever need me."

"I haven't needed you before. What makes you think I would need you now?"

He appeared crestfallen. Did he really think she'd jump at the chance to stay in touch when they hadn't for years?

"Daniella—"

"Oh, wait, you *did* pay child support." While his sons had his love and affection, she hadn't received even a birthday card from him since her eighth birthday, after he married the woman he'd been having an affair with behind her mother's back. "So I should thank you for that. I should also thank you for covering my mother's medical bills after she died, but I was more than capable of doing it." It would have been a financial strain. She would have covered the bills, though, but he beat her to it.

"I wanted to," he said. "It was the least I could do."

"Do you think it somehow makes up for the way you discarded her?" *The way you discarded me?* she wanted to scream.

"No, I don't."

He looked pitiful, and she didn't want to feel sorry for him. "Goodbye, Carlos." Daniella rose from the table.

"I never deserted you," he said hastily. "No matter what you think." His voice halted her with her back turned to him.

She whirled around in anger. "Don't you lie to me," she hissed. "You had your new wife and your new family, and that's all that mattered." His sons had gone into business with him. Since he'd sold the business and moved to Miami, what were they doing now? No doubt living off the millions of dollars her father had earned over the years. Twiddling their thumbs as they chased women around the globe. From what she understood from other family members, her younger siblings were quite the playboys. They'd taken after their father. She lifted her chin and looked down at him with disdain. "I don't need you for anything. I don't need your money, your time, nothing. You didn't want me, but it didn't stop me from being successful."

A pained expression crossed his face and he reached a hand to her but only caught air. "That's not true. I wanted you, and I'm so proud of everything you've accomplished."

"Why would you be proud? You had absolutely nothing to do with my success. I'm successful in spite of your rejection." She should be quiet. Otherwise she'd say too much and he'd guess how much his absence had truly affected her. How devastated she'd been for years when she realized he was never coming back. She would never get another piggyback ride. He would never introduce her to another person as his favorite girl and the best thing in his life.

She could never treat her own child in such a cruel manner. She knew the pain of rejection, and her child would not grow up doubting the love of either of its parents. She'd already taken steps to ensure that didn't happen.

Carlos stood. "I know you don't need me, but I'm your father, and no matter what you believe, I loved you. I still do." He paused, then reached into his pocket. "My contact information, in case you ever change your mind and want to get in touch."

He tried to hand her the card, but she didn't take it. The truth was, she couldn't move. The memories that had tormented her flooded back like a burst dam, and she was afraid if she moved a muscle she might collapse completely. Then he'd know the truth.

Very carefully, he placed the card on the table. "I'm staying at the Four Seasons Hotel until Saturday if you want to meet up again and talk."

"I won't."

He nodded. "I understand. Goodbye, baby girl."

He had no right to call her that. The softly spoken endearment pierced her cold armor, but fortunately he'd already started toward the door.

She bit her trembling lip and blinked to fight back the tears. A man at a nearby table openly watched her, and she lowered her gaze, blinking rapidly against the tears flooding her eyes. When her blurry vision cleared, her eyes focused on the card he'd left behind.

Simple and white with black letters, it listed his name, address, and cell phone number. She stared at it for a long time. She didn't know how long she stood there, lost in her own world, remembering how every birthday came and went. Christmas came and went. Every holiday, every summer, *every single day*, passed, and she never heard from her father.

Maybe if she hadn't known how wonderful having him in her life could be it wouldn't have hurt so much. But she'd been eight years old when he disappeared, and she still remembered all the fun times they'd had. He'd taken her fishing, and he even took her down to the work sites with him and put a hard hat on her head so she could safely walk through the buildings he renovated. She'd been a daddy's girl for sure.

Then he disappeared, as if he'd fallen off the edge of the world. When he'd divorced her mother, he'd divorced her, too. He hadn't broken one heart. He'd broken two.

She picked up the card and tore it into tiny pieces. Then she took the pieces and walked over to the trash receptacle and tossed them in. Nothing had changed, and she'd turned out fine. She didn't need him then and she certainly didn't need him now.

CHAPTER ELEVEN

One of the drawbacks to his position in life was the number of events Cyrus had to attend. Political functions, charity functions, fundraisers, and all manner of social engagements. The list seemed endless. He'd cut back in recent years, but he still showed up to quite a few on a regular basis. At least this event was different. His sister was happy and getting married.

The majority of people at the engagement party were family and Ivy's friends, which meant he didn't have to suffer through pitches to invest in the next hot business idea, mothers practically throwing their daughters at him—despite the fact that he wore his ring and was still married—nor be forced to make conversation, because most everyone here knew small talk wasn't his forte.

Situated on Lake Union, the grounds of Cyrus's mother's estate had been transformed into a colorful display in celebration of Ivy and Lucas's engagement. Bright colors dominated the decorations, and tulips—his mother and Ivy's favorite flower—had been imported from the Netherlands and adorned the white-linen covered tables in bright reds, oranges, and purples. Upon entering, guests received white note cards with *Advice for the Bride & Groom* engraved in gold letters, with the expectation they would write their advice on the lines below and drop them in a glass box sitting on a table by itself.

Plenty of squealing and hugging took place as guests arrived to celebrate with the future bride and groom. Lucas didn't have any family members in attendance because he didn't know his family, but everyone at the party took the opportunity to get to know him and make him feel welcomed.

In addition to chairs and tables set up on the grass, there were stations laden down with more than enough food and beverages. One table had heavy hors d'oeuvres and another was piled high with cakes and cookies. A Bloody Mary station allowed guests to build their own unique version of the drink, and the family's Full Moon beer was available in abundance. For nondrinkers like Cyrus, one station offered nonalcoholic beverages.

Standing on the perimeter of the festivities with his brother, Trenton, Cyrus's eyes rested on Daniella, chatting with a guest over near the drinks table. He could hardly take his eyes from her. She wore her hair loose around her shoulders, the way he liked, and she managed to make the simple long skirt and oversized peasant top she wore look like high fashion. To him, she was the most beautiful woman in attendance. Today she was returning home, and he could hardly wait. He could almost feel those long legs wrapped around him, her soft body clinging to his in rapturous release, and his ass clenching under the bite of her fingernails.

A scream pierced the air. Like everyone else, Cyrus turned toward the sound and saw Ivy with her hand over her mouth. He followed her wide-eyed gaze to see his brother, Gavin, coming down the stone steps that led from the back of the house.

The prodigal son had returned.

Cyrus couldn't see his brother's eyes behind the dark-tinted aviator sunglasses, but Gavin smiled fondly at his sister as she rushed forward into his arms. He lifted her off the ground and swung her around in two full circles. Once everyone realized there was nothing to be alarmed about, a low hum of excited chatter started.

Cyrus couldn't hear what his brother and sister were saying, but the happiness on Ivy's face conveyed her joy at seeing her twin.

"Would you look at that," Trenton murmured. He took a carrot stick from the crudité cup he held and crunched it. "I didn't think he would come."

"I guess he thought better of it," Cyrus said.

Trenton eyed him suspiciously. "What did you do?"

"I reminded him of how important his presence is to his sister."

That and threatening to cut him off financially had done the trick. As the executor of their father's will, Cyrus was responsible for the allowances paid out to all family members. Since Gavin didn't work, he depended on his allowance to finance his partying around the world.

Trenton laughed. "Yeah right. Whatever you did, it worked. Mother's happy, too," he added as their mother hurried over to envelope her son in her arms.

Friends and family greeted Gavin with enthusiastic hugs and smiles, many of whom hadn't seen him in years, so it was a while before he made his way to them. When he finally did, he sauntered over.

"Good to see you, bro." Trenton gave him a hug and they slapped each other on the back.

Cyrus's lips quirked into a smile. "Changed your mind, I see," he said.

"I guess you're happy." Gavin shoved the glasses atop his head. "I'm going to get you back for this."

"For telling you to come home? I'm not losing any sleep over your threats. Stay a while. For some reason Mother and Ivy want you here and are glad to see you. Look how happy they are, although I have no idea why."

Gavin laughed. His light brown eyes, the same color as their father's, crinkled in the corners. The contrast with his dark brown skin was the first thing women noticed about him and made them practically swoon. Cyrus sometimes thought Gavin wore sunglasses so often to make the reveal of his eyes more dramatic.

"Tell the truth, you're happy to see me, too. That's why you wanted me here so badly."

"Don't flatter yourself."

Gavin laughed again. "I might stay a while if I can find a way to occupy my time." He looked around at the attendees. "What's the scoop on the ladies?" He directed the question to Trenton.

"You don't waste any time, do you?" Cyrus asked dryly.

"Unlike you, I'm not in any hurry to get married. You are still married, aren't you?"

"Barely," Trenton answered.

"And where is the lovely Daniella? That woman should be nominated for sainthood for putting up with you for as long as she did. Are you ever going to give her a divorce?"

Both his brothers looked at him and waited for an answer.

"We've recently reconciled. Worry about your own love life and not mine," he told his brothers.

"My love life is great, as always," Gavin said. "So who are the single ladies?"

Trenton pointed them out with his chin. "That one over there is recently divorced. The one in the cream dress will be happy to see you. Every time she sees me she asks about you."

"What's her name again?"

"Sharon."

"Oh yeah, Sharon." Gavin licked his lips and smiled. "What about her, in the gray skirt?"

"That's Alannah," Cyrus answered. Trenton's best friend.

"I couldn't tell with her back to us." Gavin shifted his gaze to Trenton and then back at Alannah, who'd now turned around and was in conversation with their mother. "What's up with you and her? The two of you still just friends?"

"Don't go there," Cyrus warned.

"She's more than a friend. She's family," Trenton said.

"She ain't my family," Gavin said. "I'm just asking a question. The two of you still platonic? Because if you are, I might take a shot at her. I've always thought she was kind of cute."

Cyrus anticipated the impending explosion as Gavin purposely baited Trenton.

"Cut it out. She's a good girl." The note in Trenton's voice had grown harder.

"You're a better man than me," Gavin continued. He kept his eyes on Alannah. "She's got the nerdy librarian thing going on with the glasses and the bun. If I hadn't seen Alannah in a bathing suit when she came on vacation with us, I'd swear she didn't have a body under those oversized clothes. Makes me want to take them off and find out how—"

Trenton walked up to his brother and stood nose to nose with him. "Enough."

Gavin put up his hands with a laugh. "I can't pay your friend a compliment? Calm down, I'm kidding."

"It's not funny. She's a nice girl. Show some respect."

The stare off ended when Trenton stepped back and looked out at the lake. Gavin locked eyes with Cyrus.

"I told you," Cyrus said with a shrug.

Gavin patted Trenton on the shoulder. "I'm sorry, all right? I didn't come home to create problems. I came to celebrate my sister getting engaged and meet the guy she's supposed to marry. Let's forget I said anything about the nice and sweet Alannah." He flung his arm around Trenton's neck.

Trenton didn't hug him back. "You play too damn much."

Gavin grinned to neutralize his brother's anger. "Come on. Introduce me to the women who aren't so nice. Those are the ones I really want to meet." With his hand still around Trenton's neck, he hauled his younger brother with him toward a couple of women.

"Those two together will mean nothing but trouble," a voice said. Xavier had walked over with a drink in his hand. As usual, he didn't dress the part of a wealthy man. He never wore name brand anything, and today had on a plain shirt and jeans. His dreads were pulled back from his face in a thick ponytail.

Cyrus nodded his agreement. "I feel like I should issue a warning to all the women here."

Xavier didn't respond, but Cyrus could tell he wanted to talk. They stared after their brothers as they chatted up two of Ivy's friends standing over by one of the tables.

"You look tired. You need to get some rest," Xavier said.

"Somebody has to put in the long hours. You wouldn't know anything about that, though, would you?"

Xavier bit his lip in annoyance, as if biting back harsh words. Shaking his head, he shot his brother an angry look. "I'm tired of your cracks about the work I do. You've never respected it, but it's work, even if you don't think so." Working with nonprofits, he brought attention to the economic inequalities in resource-rich African countries.

"Not the work you were meant to do."

"What was I meant to do, Cyrus?" He lowered his voice because he'd gotten rather loud. "I'm not you, okay? I was never the CEO type. Father knew that. It's why he left you in charge. You're practically a clone of him." He said the last with disgust, which made Cyrus straighten and stare at him. "Do you even know who you are—outside of being Cyrus Junior?"

"Who else would I be?"

"You have his name, his responsibility, and that's all you have. Do you have any friends? When was the last time you took the boat out on the lake and relaxed? When was the last time you took a vacation? You sit on your throne on top of Mount Johnson and use money to control everything and everyone. He groomed you well."

Cyrus laughed softly, mildly amused by his brother's sanctimonious pronouncements.

"While you're complaining about the money, what about you, Xavier? Who are you? Why do you feel the need to hide who you are, with the dreadlocks and the bargain basement clothes? You're trying so hard to be somebody else, to hide from your wealth while still collecting a nice check every month."

"I hardly spend a dime of my allowance," Xavier grated. "What I do spend helps others in my nonprofit work."

"And the money finances your trips, doesn't it? A few years ago, when you were stuck in a Senegalese prison, it was the money from Mount Johnson that got you freed." Cyrus looked around at the smiling guests. "I don't understand why you can't work at the company our father worked so hard to build."

"Not everyone is cut out for business, and there's more to life than money."

"Why can't you do both? Save the world and work at the company?" Cyrus said. "Why are you so ashamed of who you are and where you came from? Do you know how many people would love to be you?"

"Of course I do. Do you know how many people suffer everyday because they don't have enough to eat and because of corporations like ours, underpaying and raping resources from local communities? The rich getting richer and the poor poorer."

"Save me the tired clichés," Cyrus said with a wave of his hand. "Your statistics say one thing, mine say there's a growing middle class, and it's larger than ever before."

"Anyone can doctor numbers to coincide with their arguments. I don't trust your funny math."

"And I should trust yours?"

"We'll never see eye to eye on this," Xavier pronounced. He

looked ready to move on.

"Not as long as you continue to run from your birthright."

"My birthright?" Xavier said bitterly, swinging back in his direction. "The only person Father thought was good enough to run the company was you, and he was ridiculously tough on all of us."

"Tough but fair."

"No, just tough. He groomed you to be the next him. It's so embroiled in you, you don't even have a separate identity. It started with the name. No one can tell anymore that you have your own personality because you *are* him, and because of that, you were his favorite, the crown prince of the Johnson empire."

"So jealousy is the reason you've abandoned your responsibility to help run the company?" Cyrus demanded. He'd known for a while that Xavier held resentment toward him, but he'd never been certain of the cause.

"Did he ever ask *you*, 'Why can't you be more like your brother?'" Xavier snapped. He stopped, as if he'd revealed too much. Then he plowed on since he'd said plenty already. "*I* never measured up."

Cyrus was bewildered by his brother's remarks. "Is that what you think?"

"It's what I know. I'm good at what I do," Xavier said. "I help people and do something meaningful with my life instead of sipping champagne around the pool all day."

"If you think that's how my day is spent, you're wrong," Cyrus said dryly.

"Everyone knows how hard you work, Cyrus," Xavier said in a grudging tone.

Cyrus stared out at the guests, not really seeing them. All he saw was his father lying in the hospital bed, giving Cyrus his last instructions to take care of the family and keep the Johnson name clean. To continue building on the family's success so future generations could benefit. They were tasks Cyrus took very seriously.

"You're wrong about Father," he said. "He wanted you to work for the company. He wanted you and me to be side by side, running everything. He trusted you."

Xavier looked at Cyrus with a mixture of curiosity and suspicion. "Why are you telling me this?"

"Because it's true. He did believe in you, but he wasn't very good at expressing himself." A trait Cyrus seemed to have inherited.

"Come on, Cyrus," Xavier said with a chuckle. "Is this one of your tactics to get what you want? You want me back here, so now you're trying to convince me Father actually wanted me to help run the company?"

Cyrus stared straight at his brother. "You know I never play games to get what I want. Father wanted us to get along and run the company together, and he was disappointed in your lack of interest."

Xavier fell silent for awhile, mulling the words. "I'm not cut out for the corporate life," he mumbled.

"Maybe you're afraid," Cyrus said.

"I'm not afraid," Xavier growled, turning to his brother with his empty hand clenched into a fist at his side. "Stop saying that."

Cyrus faced him squarely. "Then stop running away," he shot back. He glanced around to make sure they weren't drawing attention to themselves. "Bring all your save-the-world passion to Johnson Enterprises. Who knows what will happen if you and I work together. We could possibly become the number one beer company in the country." He'd thought about it at length, and it was possible. They were already in the top three, so to reach number one wasn't entirely outside the realm of possibility. He wanted to bring in consultants to help them achieve that, but if he could get Xavier in there, too, with fresh perspectives and his brilliant mind, they might be unstoppable.

"Are you saying you need me?" Xavier asked with a mocking smile.

Cyrus didn't respond right away. He thought about what Daniella had said about catching more flies with honey. He swallowed his pride. "Yes," he answered finally. "I need you."

Xavier raised his eyebrows in surprise, and then he stared down into his drink. "I'll think about it," he muttered.

CHAPTER TWELVE

Near the end of the evening, Cyrus took to the middle of the gathered group and toasted his sister and her future husband. Lucas made a toast as well, commenting on the "uneventful" progression of his and Ivy's relationship. Everyone chuckled, knowing full well the details of their dramatic reconciliation. He then recited an original poem, professing his love for Ivy and their daughter, causing a series of ooh's and ah's from the group and Ivy to wipe away tears from her eyes.

With the sun sinking, the exterior lights came on and slowly, guests started exiting. Lucas and Ivy said goodbye to each of them with hugs and kisses. Cyrus and his brothers huddled together, watching the departures. Their mother, Constance Johnson, walked over and clasped her hands in front of her. Her eyes encompassed her four sons, and her face glowed with pleasure and motherly pride. "It's so good to see all my boys here together." She patted Gavin's cheek. "I trust you're going to stay a while."

"I'm planning to," he replied. He dodged her eyes when he said it, which made Cyrus doubt his sincerity.

"Good."

She walked up to Cyrus and he bent so she could kiss his cheek.

"Thank you, dear," she said softly in his ear. "You made me and your sister very happy." She then left to help tend to the parting guests.

At least he was making someone happy. Cyrus searched for and saw his wife chatting with Ivy. A faint notch of regret swelled in his chest.

Daniella had been noticeably ill at ease during the entire party. At least to him, though others probably didn't notice. She was probably worried about tonight. He needed to think of a way to ease the transition back into married life.

****

"I have to give you another hug before I go and tell you again how happy I am for you." Daniella embraced Ivy.

Ivy beamed at her. "Thank you." She spread her fingers and stared at the brilliant Asscher cut diamond. Daniella's had the same cut, except hers was a huge yellow diamond. "I can't believe I'm getting married. Well, married again." Ivy was a widow.

Daniella had always gotten along with her. They'd become friends after she married Cyrus, and after they split, Ivy had told her, *"Don't be a stranger. You and I can still be friends even if you're no longer married to my brother."*

But Daniella hadn't felt right about it, and she'd cut off all contact. The last time she'd seen Ivy was at the same restaurant opening for a friend where she'd seen Cyrus. They'd spoken briefly and she'd promised to call Ivy to do lunch, but she'd never called and neither had Ivy.

"I'm so glad you're back," Ivy said with sincerity. "I hope the two of you can work it out this time. Goodness knows Cyrus needs someone to keep him in line."

"I don't think anyone can keep him in line."

Ivy's eyes filled with amusement. "True, he can be difficult, but he slowed down some after the two of you got married. We were all glad because, well…you know, after the health scare he had."

After Ivy dropped that bombshell, she hugged a family member who had approached. Daniella waited impatiently as they chatted before the woman walked away. "I didn't know Cyrus had a health scare," she said.

"You didn't? My goodness, he was in the hospital for two days. His body shut down from extreme exhaustion. We were all frantic and scared to death, of course."

Daniella's stomach lurched sickeningly. Cyrus, who was so energetic, and who she often thought of as invincible, had been laid up in a hospital bed for days. "When did this happen?"

Ivy screwed up her face in deep thought. "Um…about a year or two before he met you, I think. Yes, that's right. When you consider that he's always been an overachiever—I mean, he got his MBA from Wharton at twenty years old and started working with my father right after—I'm surprised it didn't happen sooner. After he left the hospital, he became obsessive about everything. You know how he is. He's adamant about order and maintaining control in every aspect of his life, and not long after he fell ill, he bought a house and told my mother he wanted to get married and have kids. He kicked up his exercise regimen, and he started eating better. Proper eating habits was one of the things the doctor stressed. No more skipping meals and plenty of water."

Daniella glanced across the lawn to where Cyrus stood talking to Lucas and a family member. He looked so vibrant and strong, but now she understood his almost fanatical eating and exercise habits. "He never told me."

"You know how my brother is. He's too busy taking care of everyone else, and God forbid anyone know he's actually human—made of flesh and blood like the rest of us."

Daniella had always thought of him as godlike, but knowing his health had suffered in such an extreme way made him seem… She shook her head at the silly notion he needed caring for. The danger had long passed, and Cyrus was *not* vulnerable.

"You would think his health scare would make him more compassionate toward others. The things he does to make money…" She bit her lip. She shouldn't badmouth him to his own sister, but Ivy's expression settled into one of reflection rather than condemnation.

"He can definitely be difficult," she agreed, "but his decisions aren't always cut and dry, and frankly, I'm glad he has to make the final call on most things. I sure wouldn't want to. A while back sales had declined for several years in a row. We'd all voted to keep the marketing firm in place because we thought they could turn things around. After all, my father had hired them and they'd worked with us for years, but Cyrus wasn't convinced. He made the radical decision to fire them. The truth is, it was time for them to go, and he was the only one brave enough to make the call. He found a smaller firm in Atlanta and gave them the job to create a fresh marketing campaign. It included new ads and a brand new social media strategy. Since then, sales have spiked upward again. If he hadn't made the decision to fire the first firm, we might have had to lay people off, something none of us wanted to do."

"Are you saying it wasn't about the bottom line?"

"No, Cyrus likes to make money. It's always about the bottom line." Ivy laughed. "But it's more complicated than that." She squeezed Daniella's arm. "He works hard, sometimes too hard, and not even Mother can get him to slow down. That's why I'm really glad the two of you are back together." She looked so grateful, Daniella felt a pang of guilt. She didn't plan to stay married to Cyrus. Ivy thought they had a much better relationship than they did. "You're good for him."

Good for him, Daniella mused. She'd heard that comment before from other members of the Johnson family when they first married. While she considered their words a compliment, no one seemed to consider whether or not Cyrus was good for *her*.

****

The ride home in the chauffeured sedan was quiet. Daniella stared out the window, watching the lights of the buildings go by.

"You're all moved in?" Cyrus asked beside her.

She nodded and glanced over at him. "I haven't been home yet." It felt strange to call the mansion home, but it was, for now. "Shaun assured me everything will be unpacked when I get there."

"If you're not satisfied with anything he's done, let him know and he'll fix it."

"I'm sure he did a good job," she said.

Cyrus worked his staff hard, but even she had to admit he was generous to them. They received large bonuses, not only in the form of money, but as trips abroad, cars, and jewelry. He was particularly sensitive to any familial issues among his staff. She recalled a time when Ms. Ernestine's sister had been ill, and he'd paid to have her moved to a private facility and given his housekeeper paid time off to stay with her sister until she recovered.

"How's business?" Cyrus asked after a few minutes. He lifted his hand to forestall her response, and quickly added, "I'll just listen."

A smile tugged at the corner of her mouth, and she gave in to it. They used to talk about business late at night. She'd tell him her concerns and what she worried about. Then he'd make suggestions of what she could do to fix the problems. At times she found it aggravating, but then she realized he was one of those men—the kind who saw a problem and had to fix it. He couldn't help himself. She learned to preface every conversation with the words, "I just need you to listen."

"Business is good," she said, staring at her fingers, "but there's a lot going on."

"Like what?"

She eyed him warily. She desperately wanted to confide in someone. But could she trust him?

He shifted in the seat. "I can tell by the way you answered there's more you want to say."

Very perceptive, as usual. In all honestly, she felt overwhelmed. Seeing her father had added another layer to the stress in her life. Between fighting with Cyrus, working on the business plan, and seeing her father, it was a wonder she hadn't drunk more than one Bloody Mary at the party.

"Beaux-Arts Galleries is expanding to Manhattan, and I'm a little stressed, I guess. We're growing so fast, and um…" She chewed on her upper lip. "I'm nervous about it," she said quietly.

Embarrassed, she could feel his eyes on her but she refused to look at him. She'd said too much.

"The bigger you get, the more responsibility there will be," Cyrus said.

"I suppose."

"You sound doubtful," he said.

"Sometimes I have my doubts." She crossed her arms over her chest and stared out the window. She'd never admitted her fears to anyone, and since Cyrus was so confident in his abilities, he would only see her insecurities as weakness.

"I promise not to tell you what to do, but I'll tell you a quick story." In the dim interior, the pools of his dark brown eyes were thoughtful as he searched for the right words. "One day my father told me I would be responsible for the launch of our seasonal beer. I was fresh out of graduate school and it was the first time he'd ever given me complete control over a product launch. I was worried I'd fail, and I told him. At the time he told me something I'll never forget. 'If you're not a little scared, then you're not thinking big enough. Nothing, not even failure, should stop your progress.' Remember that, Dani. You can do anything you put your mind to."

Her throat constricted at his words of encouragement. "I didn't know you felt that way."

"I've always thought you were smart. That's one of the traits that attracted me to you."

Now she was confused. "But you were so adamant about having a child on a specific timeline, I thought…I thought you'd expect me to give up my gallery."

"Why would you think that?" Cyrus frowned. "Having a baby and having a career are not mutually exclusive. I never asked you to stop working. I know how much you enjoy your work and how important it is to you. You wanted your gallery to be one of the best on the west coast, and it is. Now you're on your way to make waves on the east coast. I'm proud of you."

Her father had said the same thing, but for some reason Cyrus's words held more value. She appreciated his words in a way she'd never expected.

With a tilt of her head she considered him. "You know what I want. What do you want, Cyrus?" she asked.

"Whatever my wife wants," he quipped.

"That can't be all," she said, refusing to let him off the hook. Based on what Ivy had told her at the party, she expected him to say he wanted a child. She knew that had to be the most important thing to him.

"No, that's not all I want," he said quietly.

"Then what?" Disconcerted by the thought she might not really know him at all, Daniella desperately wanted an answer to get insight into his character.

His eyes didn't leave hers. "I want you to be happy."

The way he said it, she almost believed him.

CHAPTER THIRTEEN

Daniella took a deep breath. She looked calm enough in the bathroom mirror in her white silk dressing gown. She knotted the belt, unraveled it, and then knotted it again—tighter this time.

She was alone because Cyrus had decided to do a walk-through of the house first before joining her upstairs. She'd used the time alone to freshen up and get dressed for bed. It felt silly to be so nervous, but she couldn't help it. They hadn't had sex in a long time, and if she were honest, the feeling in the pit of her stomach wasn't only jitters but rather a fifty-fifty blend of jitters and heightened anticipation.

She pulled open one of the drawers and pulled the pack of birth control pills from the back. She popped one out and dry-swallowed, then hid the package in the back again. She didn't look at herself in the mirror. She wasn't proud of the decision she'd made, but bringing a child into a marriage that would eventually break apart was not an option. All she had to do was get past the six month mark, and then she could get her divorce. She knew Cyrus would keep his word.

When she exited the bathroom, she half expected to see him, but the room was quiet and he was nowhere in sight. No light under his bathroom door, so clearly he hadn't come upstairs yet. She stood uncertainly in the middle of the room, unsure what to do. Would he expect her to be waiting naked in bed for him, or did he have seduction in mind tonight?

She was about to slide into bed when the door opened and Cyrus walked in. He raised an eyebrow at her appearance and the sensation in her stomach deepened.

"In a bit of a hurry, aren't you? The night's still young." He began to unbutton his shirt.

"I didn't know what you expected or what timeframe you're on."

"As much as I anticipate making love to you, have looked forward to it for days…" His voice drifted low with longing, causing a wave of sweltering heat to fan over her skin. "I've decided we're going to take things slow."

The unexpected declaration left her speechless for several seconds. "What?"

"That's right. In fact, I won't be touching you anytime soon."

"Excuse me?" Not only surprise filled her voice. Could he hear the disappointment, too?

"When we make love, you'll have to initiate it."

He'd completed unbuttoning his shirt and it hung open to reveal a stretch of toned chocolate skin. Her eyes remained riveted there for an inappropriately long time.

She lifted her eyes to his and cleared her throat. "I didn't even want this reconciliation, and you think I'll *initiate* sex?"

"You never had problems initiating sex before. I remember you were quite adventurous, to the point where you'd interrupt my work from time to time."

She remembered, too, and heat burned her cheeks. A few times she'd gone down to his home office and convinced him to set aside work long enough to pay her some needed attention.

"That was before," she pointed out. Before their marriage fell apart and everything between them changed. "I happen to have self-control."

Cyrus shrugged, appearing nonchalant. "So do I."

"*You're* going to go six months without sex?"

"I don't think it'll take that long, but why not?" He pulled off the shirt on his way to his bathroom. The firm muscles of his chest moved under his smooth dark skin. His body was even harder and firmer than she remembered, his waist trim and taut, and his stomach a flat washboard of grooved muscles. She bit her lip in amazement. He'd certainly been taking good care of himself. "I've already done three years. What's six more months?" he asked.

He disappeared into the bathroom, leaving a stunned Daniella behind. He hadn't had sex in three years? Impossible, surely. He had remained faithful and honored their vows all this time? She sank onto the edge of the bed.

Once again he'd surprised her.

****

A cold spray of water pelted Cyrus's body from the overhead fixture. He must be out of his damn mind, but the thought had come to him as he made his rounds to check the property. His house manager usually performed that task, but he'd needed a break from Daniella to clear his head. When the chauffeur drove through the gate, lusty imaginings of having his wife beneath him had kicked up until he could barely think straight.

He wanted her badly. In fact, seeing her in that white dressing gown, the silk draped lovingly over her ample breasts, had almost been his undoing, but he was nothing if not disciplined. He would prove to her he could be trusted, that he was the kind of man she could be proud to call her husband, in the same way he was proud to call her his wife.

Cyrus lifted his head to the icy spray, appealing to the frigid temperature to erase the hard-on standing straight up from his hips.

Unfortunately, he had insisted they share a bed. It would be torture, but he planned to stick to his decision. Even if it meant taking a cold shower every damn night.

****

Two weeks passed and Cyrus still hadn't tried to make love to her. Two whole weeks. Silently fuming, Daniella sipped her coffee, watching him over the brim of the mug.

Across the table, he devoured a breakfast of Canadian bacon, three eggs, and a stack of pancakes able to satisfy two sumo wrestlers. He had an immense appetite, but he never packed on an ounce of fat because of his workout routine, his passion for exercise as substantial as his passion for sex. Which was why his behavior stumped her. He still hadn't made a move to make love to her, but she thought about it constantly, even dreamed about it.

She'd become way too preoccupied with thoughts of him, and being around him all the time didn't help. She was actually glad when he had to work late since that gave her a little reprieve from the longing, the unbearable wanting that consumed her night and day.

The hardest moments came at night. He'd come out of the shower smelling of soap and clean with a towel wrapped around his lean waist, and she'd have to tear her eyes away from the tight musculature of his abs. Sometimes she even forgot to breathe as she watched him get dressed and would dip into her own bathroom to hide her flushed cheeks and finally get a good breath. Night after night they lay next to each other, not touching, he on one side of the bed and she on the other. He never reached for her. He barely even looked in her direction.

He'd demanded she come back so he could ignore her?

She stifled a sigh and set her mug on the table and admitted that wasn't exactly the case. During the week he stayed busy, and while some nights they'd eaten dinner together, he typically worked long hours. On the weekends, however, he'd actually taken her out on dates. Last night they'd flown to Los Angeles to have dinner at a celebrity hotspot she'd happened to mention a few days before. How he'd secured a reservation on such short notice was not a mystery. The Johnson name opened doors.

True to form, Cyrus had walked in like a celebrity himself, was shown a well-appointed table, and then they'd spent the night enjoying a multi-course meal that could only be described as an out-of-this-world dining experience. Her mouth still watered when she thought about the tender steak cooked to perfection, roasted vegetables, and a wine so perfect she'd purchased several bottles to bring back to Seattle.

The night had been pleasurable, and she'd had certain…expectations when they arrived at home. Yet once they'd climbed into bed, he'd given her a chaste kiss on the cheek and then rolled over and gone to sleep.

His indifference annoyed her.

Cyrus looked up at Daniella from his now empty plate. Tendrils of smooth, dark hair brushed her cheeks and kissed her shoulders before falling down her back. "What are your plans today?" he asked.

What would she do if he kissed her—the kind of kiss that would have her flushed and breathless? He'd learned the true meaning of blue balls the past couple of weeks. Their lack of intimacy drove fantasies through his mind at a constant rate, and kissing her on the cheek last night had only made the situation worse.

Day after day he worked out hard—harder than ever, trying not to crack. At this rate, he'd soon turn his entire body into one giant muscle.

"I'm going to the gallery to get some work done." She stood and walked over to the coffee pot. She took a travel mug from one of the cabinets. "I guess you'll be working in your office?"

"For most of the day," he admitted.

He stood as well and watched her pour coffee into the container. She appeared composed and calm, and his resolve wavered. Maybe he'd made a mistake and should satiate the ever-present need for her that hummed through his body. The idea was starting to look better and better.

He placed his dishes in the sink.

She screwed the top on the mug and said, "I'll see you later, then."

They moved at the same time. His arm bumped her breast, and he heard her sharp intake of air. A simple apology should have sufficed, but untempered desire raged through him and he caught her by the arms.

They both froze.

They stared at each other. Tension, familiar and unwelcome, tightened his shoulders.

His hands contracted around her soft skin. He could take her now. If he lifted her against the wall and dragged aside her panties, he could be inside of her within seconds without a single objection. The evidence of her own brittle resolve was laid bare in her eyes, but he'd made a promise and intended to keep it.

Somehow he managed to reel in the hunger and go against his protesting body. Somehow he managed to release her and step back.

"Excuse me," he mumbled.

She breathed through her mouth. "No problem." She swallowed and averted her eyes before rushing off.

He watched her leave. She was being extremely polite—they both were, but the tension between them had heightened. It was only a matter of time before one of them cracked under the strain.

CHAPTER FOURTEEN

Daniella awoke in the middle of the night to find Cyrus's hands on her body. In the near darkness, they roamed over her thighs and ass.

"What are you doing?" she asked breathlessly.

His mouth was against her neck. "You came over here. I have to assume this is what you want."

Indeed, she could see half the bed in front of her, and she lay wedged up against Cyrus with a hot throb between her legs. She'd had another erotic dream. This time her subconscious self had sought him out and sent her to his side of the bed.

He cupped her breasts through her nightgown, squeezing as if judging their texture. Heat swept across her skin and she trembled, thoroughly aroused as if foreplay had started hours ago. She twisted restlessly as he feathered his thumbs over the tips of her nipples. His hands felt so good she wanted the flimsy, gossamer barrier removed. She wished she could tear it off to enjoy the touch of his hands on her bare skin. Arching her back, she thrust her breasts against his palms. A helpless moan—a sound filled with unbearable yearning—spilled from her chest.

"Missed these," he groaned.

He continued to fondle her, plucking her nipples and squeezing his favorite part of her anatomy. He pressed her breasts together and slipped a hard leg between her thighs, grinding his erection into her backside. The motion evoked erotic sensations and spread fire through her veins, making her ache to have him inside of her as soon as possible.

She turned onto her back, and he rolled on top of her. The familiar weight of him pressed her into the mattress. Chest to chest, she felt the heavy thud of his heart against hers. Their rapid beats appeared to be synchronized.

She cupped the back of his head, brought his mouth down, and parted her lips, an open invitation as she readied for his tongue, anxious for a taste. A drugging kiss ensued, leisurely yet devouring, hungry yet affectionate. Their mouths slid over each other, moist and warm. He tugged her bottom lip between his teeth and nibbled softly, then moved lower to suck gently on her chin.

"Is this what you want?" he whispered against her arched throat. "Tell me."

"Yessss," she said in a sibilant whisper. "I want you." Manicured fingers moved over the fine curls on his head, scraping his scalp in a silent cry of relief that her need would soon be satisfied. He'd made her wait so long, made her suffer night after night.

"Killing me the past few weeks," he muttered, sounding almost angry. He nipped her shoulder with his teeth. "I exercised like a madman, and when exercise wasn't enough, I took matters into my own hands."

She felt a little thrill that he'd pleasured himself to thoughts of her. Happy she hadn't been alone in her torment, she whispered, "I did, too."

He groaned against her neck and pushed away the straps of her nightgown to lavish kisses on her throat and shoulders. Everywhere his mouth touched, it set her skin on fire. "It's nothing like the real thing."

He hooked his fingers in the waistband of her panties and worked them lower, slowly. His mouth followed the same path. It brushed over the hair between her legs, and she gasped at the fleeting pleasure. His tongue trailed along her inner thigh until he'd dragged the silky material down her feet, where he nibbled on her ankles and kissed her soles.

It was as if he wanted to shower affection on every single part of her body, and she welcomed the thoroughness, urging him on with husky, appreciative noises.

The rest of their clothes came off even faster. His pajama bottom and her nightgown were tossed aside to form a pile on the floor.

His fingertips skimmed the curls at the juncture of her thighs. She jerked, her nerves raw and sensitive, her every thought concentrated on that one spot. Air hissed through his teeth when he encountered the wetness there, and she closed her eyes to savor his touch. He parted the tender flesh between her legs and slid his digits through the moisture. She squirmed beneath his probing touch and grabbed at his hand, silently begging for relief. She wanted more, and he must have understood. First one, then two fingers entered the wet opening. She gloried in the intimate exploration, lifting into the thrusting motion.

"Stop playing with me," she panted.

His lips curled into a smile against her skin, and smug laughter tickled the side of her neck. Daniella kissed his jaw and ran her hands over his sculpted chest and the firm muscles of his arms. He had an incredible physique, and she couldn't get enough of touching him.

"Lower," he directed. "I want to feel your hands on me."

Daniella closed her hand around his impressive length. He was firm and hot in her palm. She started with a feather-light touch, grazing the smooth, hard skin of his shaft.

"Harder," he muttered, pushing with vigor against her fingers.

She tightened her clasp and stroked him until his breathing fractured and his belly trembled.

"Just like that," he said, his voice sounding strained and husky. His hips slid back and forth in a counter motion, while his lips dipped to an engorged nipple and pulled it into his mouth. He concentrated his attention there for some time, swirling the tip of his tongue around it, sending a direct message to her clit.

She tightened her grasp even more and pulled, tugged, until he could no longer take the contact and wrenched her hand free. "Keep this up, and you'll make me unload all over your pretty breasts."

"Do it," she whispered. She'd let him come on her breasts and ass before. She couldn't imagine allowing another man such liberties. Only Cyrus. The act added a raw, dirty element to sex, one she'd surprisingly enjoyed.

"You're a naughty girl," Cyrus said with a wicked smile. He took each of her hands and stretched her arms above her head. "But that's not how I want you tonight. This is how I want you."

He positioned his hips between her legs and she opened, eager and ready to receive him. No other sensation on earth was as pleasurable as Cyrus's virile body taking possession of hers. She closed her eyes tight, anticipating the flood of sensation.

He breeched the entrance to her body, easing in slowly so she could get used to him again. With a tremulous whimper, she lifted her pelvis to his, but he was going so slow. He rolled his hips in a merciless grind, his pelvis stroking her clit and making her wetter, as if her body wept from the sheer pleasure of it.

"Open for me," he instructed. "Open wide for your man." His movements remained slow and sure, driving her out of her mind with the steady, sexy rhythm. She did as he asked, and he leaned down to speak into her ear. "Good girl. Just like that."

The words of praise shot heat straight to her loins, sending her arousal into the stratosphere. She lifted her hips higher, taking all his length, moaning in satisfaction as his fullness rubbed against her sensitive walls.

She whispered his name, then cried it, over and over.

"That's it. Say my name," he panted. "Scream it." His hands tightened on her wrists and his thrusts became more aggressive. "You know how I love that shit." His knees opened to spread her wider. Their passion mounted, the intensity creating a tight coil in her stomach. "You know what you do to me, don't you, Dani? Dani…Dani…"

The intensity of their lovemaking never disappointed. She wrapped her legs around his waist, drawing him further into her silken heat. She pumped her hips with more urgency, and he rocked forward with a faster tempo, intensifying the pulse between her thighs. He went deep, his breaths nothing but shallow gasps.

He was relentless now he had her where he wanted her. With nothing to hold onto, her hands tightened into tense fists, her body rocking beneath his as he alternated between shallow and deep thrusts.

A deep climax shot from her core and burst free. She tightened and arched beneath him, her breath coming in short painful explosions as she was dragged through a cloud of ecstasy that left her momentarily dazed. Intense pleasure tightened her throat. As the remnants of the orgasm wrung the last bit of energy from her body, Cyrus continued to pump his hips. Gasping, his chest heaving, his movements became even more frenzied. Then he thrust once, twice, three times. He froze on the last as he discharged inside of her, a strangled noise deep in his larynx.

"Dani." He always said her name at the end, a helpless breath of a sound that told her loud and clear how deeply their lovemaking affected him.

She slipped her wrists from his weakened hands, and with his warm breath against her collarbone, she slid her hand up and down his damp back. Tight muscles reacted to her touch, and a tremor ran through him before he rolled onto his side and gathered her close.

Vaguely, she heard him murmur something, but she was too

dazed, too spent to comprehend. Her eyes drifted close, forcing her to rest. She didn't have a choice, really. She knew her husband. Since he hadn't had sex in three years, he would do his damndest to make up for it tonight.

And she had every intention of keeping up with him.

CHAPTER FIFTEEN

Daniella awoke to a dark room and soft, plush sheets and covers. *She'd had sex with her husband.* Had spent all night doing it, in fact, and loved every minute. Her nerve endings were raw and her muscles ached somewhat, but she smiled from the memories.

She rolled over in the huge bed and stared at the empty space beside her. She stretched her arm and the sheets felt cool, which meant Cyrus had been gone for awhile. He was probably on his weekend run, per usual.

She rolled into the spot he'd vacated and buried her face in the pillow. The scent of him remained there, and she reveled in it, the same as she had last night. She could stay there all day, indulging in his manly aroma. Instead, she slipped naked from the bed and went into her bathroom to put on a lightweight robe. She brushed her teeth and then went downstairs.

It was Sunday, which meant Ms. Ernestine was off. Daniella didn't bother making coffee because Cyrus wouldn't drink any. He had an aversion to anything remotely like a drug. She poured herself a glass of orange juice and searched the cabinets and refrigerator for items to make breakfast.

All of the canned and jarred goods in the cabinet had the label facing outward, and like items were grouped together. Another one of Cyrus's quirks. Thanks to Ms. Ernestine, he hadn't driven her crazy with his OCD. The housekeeper made sure the kitchen was organized in the exact order he wanted.

It wasn't long before Cyrus came in from his run, sweating and breathing heavily. His shorts showed off his tight, muscular calves from years of running. Morning stubble shadowed his jaw and gave him a raw, sexy look.

"Good morning," he said, watching her, as if he couldn't believe she was actually there, making breakfast.

"Good morning." She waited for him to say something else, perhaps mention last night and gloat about the fact that she'd initiated sex—in her sleep, no less. Subconscious or not, she'd wanted him and made the first move.

But he didn't gloat. He came close and with a hand at her waist, pulled her in for a kiss. She didn't pull away, even though he was sweaty and musty. The kiss was quick and more of a greeting by the way their mouths quickly touched before he withdrew.

He swiped sweat from his face with a forearm and then pulled a bottled water from the refrigerator. She could feel his eyes on her while he drank it.

She broke an egg into a glass bowl.

"What's for breakfast?" he asked.

"Omelets." She cracked another egg.

"While I was running, I had a thought," he said. "Ivy thinks I should take a vacation. My whole family does, actually." Knowing him, he probably should. He took his role as head of the family and the company very seriously and was the kind of person who thought if he wanted something done right, he had to do it himself. Which meant he seldom took time off.

"Are you planning to take one?" Daniella asked.

"I think we should both take one," he replied. "We should go back to Spain."

She paused. They'd gone there for their honeymoon, but the trip had been cut short because of business. She'd loved the location and often thought about it. "Back to Costa del Sol?" she asked hopefully.

"That's what I was thinking. Can you take the time off?"

"Yes, but can you?"

"I have a few business trips to take first, but I'll be able to in a few weeks."

"How long will we be able to stay?" She was getting excited.

"How long do you want to stay?"

"A week would be nice." If not, there was no point in going. By the time they recovered from jetlag, it would be time to return.

"Then we'll stay a week."

She wanted him to promise he wouldn't let business interfere, but she didn't feel comfortable saying it. With his responsibilities, it would be hard for him to completely shut out business.

"Short of someone dying, we won't cut our trip short," he promised. He must have read her mind.

Grateful, she smiled at him, and he smiled back. Then his face slowly sobered. "I'd do anything for you. You know that, don't you?"

She didn't really know, but she was starting to think he wasn't as selfish as she'd always thought. That maybe he'd changed a little in the past three years. She was saved from answering when he reached up into the cabinet and pulled down a small jar of jalapenos.

"I like these in my omelets," he said.

"Then I'll add them," Daniella said. "By the way," she added, when he was about to walk off. "You know that's weird, don't you?"

"Jalapenos in eggs?" he asked. "That's not so weird."

She opened the door of one of the cabinets and pointed out the precise organization of the shelves. "This is not normal. It's kind of Sleeping-With-the-Enemy-ish."

He lifted an eyebrow. "You've mentioned it before. And by the way, the man in that movie was a crazy wife abuser," he pointed out.

As difficult as he was, Cyrus had not been like the man in the movie, whose physical and emotional abuse sent his wife running. "True." Daniella shoved a jar of olives behind a jar of artichokes and turned several of the bottles backward.

"Don't do that." Cyrus reached up to the shelf.

Daniella knocked away his hand. "Look at you. You can't handle it, can you?" She shouldn't tease him. She knew how much it drove him crazy, but she couldn't help it. After living together for a couple of weeks and the intimacy they'd shared last night, she was starting to feel relaxed around him, and her playfulness was a direct result.

Cyrus straightened the jars so they all lined up again. "There's a reason for this order."

"And what's that?"

"You know I don't like chaos."

"And you like to control everything," she supplied.

"If things go the way they should, it saves time," he said, ignoring her remark. "It's called efficiency."

"It's called OCD," Daniella corrected. She started whisking the eggs but paused when he started tidying up. "What are you doing?"

"Just cleaning up a bit."

"I bet you don't tidy up when Ms. Ernestine is in the kitchen." She smacked his hand with the spatula. "Out."

"That's assault."

"I said out. Don't come back until I call you for breakfast." She held up the spatula, silently threatening to hit him again.

Cyrus put his hands up, lines of amusement crossing his face. "All right, I'm going up to take a shower."

But instead of leaving, he caught her wrist with the spatula and pulled her close. Goodness, he was fast.

"You stink," she murmured, making no move to get away.

"I thought women liked it when their man was sweaty from

working out or playing sports," he said, looking down at her from lowered lids.

"Lies," Daniella said.

That didn't stop him from pulling her in and sucking on her neck. Her knees weakened and she turned her head to rub her cheek against the rough stubble on his jaw. He kissed her ear and chin, and finally her mouth. She sighed with pleasure. She loved his kisses. She'd been deprived of them for so long she'd actually forgotten how good they were, how delicious he tasted, and how enjoyable the fit of his mouth over hers.

He tugged on her lower lip with his teeth. She moaned. He could give lessons on how to kiss right.

When he withdrew, she felt a pang of disappointment. He tilted up her chin, searching her eyes. For what she didn't know.

"What?" she said uneasily, unable to remain quiet under such intense scrutiny.

"Nothing." He dropped a final kiss on her nose before walking out, and she watched him leave with a strange hitch in her chest.

Daniella started setting breakfast on the table in front of the bay window instead of the formal dining room. The plates rattled in her unsteady hands. What was happening to her? She stopped moving and placed her hands on the table to steady her nerves and the shortness of breath.

"I'd do anything for you. You know that, don't you?"

The last thing she needed to do was fall in love with Cyrus again, but when he said things like that, when he looked at her the way he did, it was so easy and so tempting to believe in him and forget his reprehensible behavior.

He bought companies and tore them apart. He bought *people* for his own selfish purposes, and he had a sense of entitlement ten miles wide. Hard to blame him when he'd grown up in such a wealthy household with the expectation that everyone would do as he commanded.

She *couldn't* fall in love with him again. It would be the epitome of foolishness. She'd seen what love could do. She'd been young at the time, but her parents' divorce had been bitter. How could the relationship of two people, whose wedding photos had displayed their love and affection for each other at one time, deteriorate into the hate fest their divorce had become?

She had to guard her heart. If she fell in love with him again, she would regret it. No doubt about it. Because love was like an insidious disease that crept up on the unsuspecting. One that, even after its cure, left the victims with lifelong scars.

****

A few weeks later, Cyrus chartered a plane to Málaga, Spain in the Costa del Sol region—the southern part of the country. Located on the Mediterranean Sea, the city was a popular vacation spot for Europeans and where Cyrus and Daniella had spent their honeymoon—a honeymoon cut short because an unforeseen business emergency had cropped up back in Seattle. This time Cyrus promised their visit wouldn't be shortened.

Despite his promise, after a jetlag-induced "nap" that lasted six hours, a phone call interrupted their lunch on the balcony of their rented villa overlooking the sandy beach. Cyrus took the call inside the bedroom and minutes later, he returned. He shot her an apologetic look, told her he was sorry, and ducked back inside.

He couldn't realistically disappear as the head of a multi-billion dollar company. Too many people depended on him. Not only immediate family, but family members working at their restaurants and the breweries, and the tens of thousands of employees across the globe.

To put his mind at ease, she went into the bedroom where he was stalking back and forth and tapped him on the shoulder. "Take care of business," she said softly. "I'll still be here when you get done."

Phone to his ear, he pulled her close and kissed her. He then took off out the door in the direction of the temporary office they'd set up, though she expected him to use it more often than she did. She heard him down the hall, his voice angry and annoyed. "What the hell is going on over there? I thought we had the Vegas deal locked up."

Daniella went back out to the balcony and watched with envy all the people sunbathing and swimming in the warm blue waters. Cyrus couldn't enjoy himself, but that didn't mean she couldn't.

She donned her white two-piece and joined the other vacationers. She spent the rest of the afternoon on the beach and met a friendly couple—Rex and Sylvia O'Ryan—originally from New York but now living in Norway. They kept her company and since she wasn't sure if Cyrus would be busy at night, too, accepted their invitation to meet for dinner later.

When she returned to the villa, Cyrus apologized again, but she assured him she wasn't upset.

"I hate I missed spending time with you," he said. "I promise that won't happen again."

He was frowning, obviously struggling with the balancing act of taking care of business and being in the present, here, with her. She walked over to him and brushed her fingers over his furrowed brow. The lines immediately disappeared.

Gazing up at him, she said, "I'm fine. I'm a big girl and I know how to entertain myself." She walked toward the bathroom to wash the sand and water from her sun kissed skin.

Before she could shut the door, Cyrus shouldered his way in. His gaze swept her body, sliding in appreciation over the slender lines. Being outside for hours had transformed her skin into a slightly darker caramel hue, showed off to perfection in the white bikini. "I like that bathing suit," he murmured, his voice rich and dark. She glanced down at the rise in his pants and smiled.

"You do, huh?"

"Mhmm." His fingers traced a line under the curve of her breast in the halter-topped bikini and her nipples puckered in response.

"What about the green one?" she asked. She'd worn it poolside in Seattle and he'd paid her plenty of compliments at the time.

"I like that one, too," he said with a slow grin that made her breath hitch. "But this is my new favorite."

He pulled at the bow behind her neck and the top fell away to reveal her breasts, her nipples turning into even harder pebbles.

"Yeah, this is my new favorite," he said. He covered her mouth and backed her toward the shower.

They undressed slowly, kissing and stroking each other in a leisurely manner, as if they had all the time in the world. And it felt as if they did. Being away from the hustle and bustle of their everyday life had slowed them down.

When they finished their shower, Daniella wasn't just washed clean. She'd been licked and kissed with a thoroughness that had sent her spiraling into two satisfying orgasms.

Chapter Sixteen

Dinner with the O'Ryans was at an open-air restaurant in Málaga, chosen for its proximity to the beach and abundant fresh seafood. While they waited for the other couple, Cyrus and Daniella perused the menu and decided on one of the special grills or *especial parilladas*, for two persons. Daniella didn't think she could eat that much food, but with Cyrus's appetite, the amount of seafood promised would probably be perfect for him.

They were chatting quietly when the O'Ryans finally arrived, both flustered as they hurried over to the table.

"Sorry for the delay," Sylvia said. She sounded out of breath, as if they'd sprinted to the restaurant from their hotel near the villa. After they were introduced to Cyrus, she said, "We left the kids with my mother-in-law, and we had a minor emergency. My youngest wasn't feeling well and wanted to talk to me. She's the baby."

"She's not a baby, but you treat her like it," Rex said with a good-natured smile. He rested his hand on the back of his wife's chair. "Our youngest is five, and ever since she turned two, my wife has been trying to convince me to have another one. To make up for it, she treats our daughter like a baby."

"I do not." Sylvia hit him on the shoulder.

Rex rubbed the spot, pretending to be hurt. "Kids are expensive, and I think four is enough, don't you?" He looked at Cyrus for agreement. He didn't know who Cyrus was. Daniella had only told them her husband hadn't been able to join her on the beach because of a business call. They had no idea the extent of Cyrus's wealth.

"I wouldn't know," Cyrus said. "We don't have any yet, but we're working on it."

Daniella took a sip of her wine. She felt a twinge of guilt over the pills she'd brought on the trip.

"How long have you been married?" Sylvia asked.

"Four years," Cyrus supplied.

"Don't rush. Enjoy each other while you can," Rex advised. "Because once the kids come, your life will be completely different."

"In a good way," Sylvia said, shooting her husband a chiding glance.

"Most of the time," he added, a mischievous glint in his eye. Their differing viewpoints were a sight to behold. They managed to disagree without being disagreeable, argue without being argumentative and mean to each other. A skill no doubt learned over their fifteen years together.

"We are looking forward to it," Cyrus said. "We're definitely ready to start a family." He slid his arm across the back of her chair.

Daniella remained silent, conflicted. He trusted her, but she had been deceiving him for weeks. And with their newfound intimacy, having a baby didn't seem like such a bad idea. Maybe they *could* make their marriage work after all.

As they sat there talking with the O'Ryans, Cyrus impressed her with his ability to switch gears. One minute he was the affable husband making small talk and discussing how he looked forward to having a family of his own. The next he spoke Spanish to the waitress and translated the conversation to the rest of them so they could better understand what was offered in each dish. She was impressed and a little jealous, regretting that she'd never learned to speak her grandmother's language.

He appeared to be quite relaxed, laughing and talking easily with the O'Ryans. He should take time off more often. The only other time she could remember seeing him like this was during their honeymoon. Perhaps the difference was because no one here knew who he was, and therefore had no expectations in regard to him. When they inquired about his business, he briefly mentioned the restaurants without giving the names, and avoided telling them about the beers. If they were curious, they didn't pry, but it was obvious he wanted to maintain his anonymity.

All of a sudden she felt the need to connect with him, and she touched his thigh with her hand under the table. The muscle there flexed, but he didn't miss a beat in the conversation. Across from her, the O'Ryans were none the wiser about what she'd done.

Feeling daring and mischievous, she squeezed his leg, wanting to unnerve him a little bit. He simply covered her hand and held it in place. She allowed him to do so for a little bit longer and joined the conversation. The O'Ryans did most of the talking, discussing their children and their antics.

Daniella slipped her hand from Cyrus's and commented on something Sylvia said. At the same time, Daniella brushed her fingers over her husband's crotch. He nodded his head at one of Rex's remarks, but her action elicited an almost unnoticeable tightening of his hand on the table. His right hand, still resting on his thigh, swiped across her mons so unexpectedly she almost leaped from her chair. She moved suddenly, and to cover her reaction, she started coughing.

"You okay?" Cyrus asked, his face filled with false concern. He rested a hand at her back.

Continuing the charade, Daniella pressed her hand to her chest and cleared her throat. "The wine went down the wrong pipe," she said, even though she hadn't touched her wine in several minutes.

"Excuse me. I need to run to the restroom."

"Hurry back," Cyrus said, his eyes filled with amusement.

Daniella knew exactly what to do to fix him. In the bathroom, she removed her underwear and balled it up in her hand. She checked her appearance briefly and smiled at the playful expression on her face. This trip had been good for them. She was actually feeling a little giddy.

She made her way back to the table and sat down.

"Feeling better now?" Cyrus asked.

"I'm feeling a bit flushed, but I'll be fine," she replied.

"Would you like some water?" Sylvia asked, already picking up the glass pitcher.

"Thank you. That would be nice." Daniella accepted the glass and took several sips before rejoining the conversation.

They'd moved on to favorite vacation spots. Rex said their trip to Australia had been his favorite, but Sylvia said their honeymoon touring southern Italy had been hers.

"How about you two?" Sylvia asked.

"I work a lot, so we haven't had much opportunity to travel together," Cyrus said. "That will change in the near future." He said it with such confidence, she didn't doubt him for a minute.

"This region is my favorite," Daniella said. "It's where we spent our honeymoon and coming here again was a good idea to re-energize our marriage."

Cyrus glanced at her and she smiled. She meant it. The different environment had caused them both to relax. Hopefully the longer they stayed the closer they'd become.

Cyrus's hand remained on his thigh, and she slipped her panties under his fingers. It took a few seconds for him to comprehend what he held. She knew the exact moment he did because he stiffened slightly and then looked briefly down at his hand. As he stuffed the black lace into his pocket, she took the opportunity to entice him further by crossing her legs and pulling her dress higher, up to mid-thigh.

He looked sharply at her. "What did you say?" he asked.

Daniella frowned at him in confusion. "I didn't—"

"It seems my wife still isn't well," Cyrus said, talking over her. He touched her forehead. "I should get her back to the villa. She feels hot." His eyes met hers, and the desire there did indeed heat her blood.

"Yes, we should probably go," she agreed, putting on as much of a pitiful face as she could, considering she wanted to burst out laughing.

"Oh no, too bad," Sylvia said. Her mouth turned down in disappointment.

"Yes, it is," Cyrus said regretfully.

He stood quickly, and the O'Ryans looked startled at the speed with which he bolted from the chair. His behavior was comical because he remained calm on the outside, but his speedy movements contradicted his tranquil exterior.

"Have dinner on us." Cyrus went for his wallet in the same pocket as her underwear. He tried to maneuver around it, but in his haste, the black lace fell onto the table.

Daniella covered her mouth to keep from laughing out loud. To his credit, Cyrus behaved as if there was nothing unusual about a thong falling out of his pocket. Completely unruffled, he calmly retrieved the scrap of fabric and stuffed it back in. Meanwhile, Sylvia flushed, her mouth partially open.

Rex had a small smile on his face and looked at Cyrus with a bit of envy and admiration. "Like I said, enjoy your freedom for as long as you can."

Daniella stood. "I'm so sorry we disrupted your meal."

"It's perfectly fine," Sylvia said, waving off the comment.

Cyrus tossed the colorful bills of currency onto the table. "Enjoy your evening," he said.

"Thank you. You, too," Rex said, a broad grin on his face.

"I plan to," Cyrus said.

The men shared a look, and then without further ado, he grasped Daniella's hand and hauled her toward the front door of the restaurant. She'd abandoned all pretense and was grinning from ear to ear. They flew down the steps as if running from a fire.

"I haven't eaten," Daniella said, laughing.

"Don't worry. I have something to fill you up."

A thrill shot through her. She loved when he used sexual innuendo. He didn't leer or smile slyly like other men. He kept the same neutral voice, as if having a perfectly normal conversation without any sexual overtones. Normally, she thought it was sexy, but today it was hilarious *and* super-sexy.

Long fingers clasped her wrist and forced her to keep time with him, but she barely managed with his long, purpose-filled strides extending over the ground in a wider arc than hers.

"Cyrus, I can't keep up. You're walking too fast."

"You started this," he reminded her.

Then he stopped abruptly and without warning picked her up and tossed her over his shoulder. Daniella squealed in surprise and glee. At the same time she placed a hand to her bottom to keep her dress from riding up and exposing her bare backside.

She laughed even harder now, hanging upside down over her husband's shoulder as he rushed along the sidewalk parallel to the beach. He maneuvered between pedestrians to get her back to the villa as expeditiously as possible, uncaring about the stares as only Cyrus could be.

This was the Cyrus most people didn't see. She loved his playfulness, and seeing this side of him made her feel as if she were in on a secret few people were privy to. As if he could let down the walls with her.

"You better not trip and fall with me. You need to slow down."

"No way. You started this," he repeated. "I'm going to finish it."

She snorted and lifted her gaze, peering through the cascade of her hair to watch the people behind them. A family of five turned around as they passed and she waved at them. Only the little boy waved back.

At the corner, Cyrus stood and turned this way and that, searching the area for a taxi. He didn't act as if he held a grown woman over his shoulder. He stood upright and wasn't even winded, like he only carried a sack filled with feathers.

He finally flagged down a taxi and they piled in. He pulled her on top of him and they made out heavily—his hand between her thighs, their mouths devouring each other. Petting and kissing like randy teenagers who had limited time to take advantage of their time alone. Or maybe it was more like horny adults on a second honeymoon.

By the time they arrived back at their temporary home, Daniella was certain she would spontaneously combust. Up on her tiptoes, she nibbled on his ear.

Cyrus pulled out a fifty euro bill and handed it to the driver. Rather than wait for the change, he pulled her toward the front door by the waist to an enthusiastic shout of *"Muchas gracias"* from the taxi.

At their door, Cyrus jammed the thin plastic into the lock slot and let them into the house, Daniella still clinging to him like a vine.

He pushed her against the wall and kissed her neck. His warm breath fanned her heated skin when he muttered, "You're in so much damn trouble."

They reached for each other at the same time, she to undo his pants and he under her dress to mold her bare bottom in his hands.

She looked up at him, and his face softened into a devilish smile that melted her heart.

I love him.

She'd run from this feeling all her life, avoided it, dodged it, because of fear of losing herself and losing her independence. Yet here she was, completely unfazed by the emotion. She laughed, oddly happy at the prospect, not even knowing or caring if he felt the same way. Right then, her heart felt so full she was certain she had enough love for the two of them.

He caught her face in his hands, studied her, and then she saw the transformation—happiness in his eyes.

"I'm glad we came back to Spain," he said.

"Me, too," she whispered back. They needed this. The trip would be a clean slate for them, a do-over. Maybe the entire reconciliation was a do-over, giving them the chance to reconnect and get to know one another again.

His mouth swooped down onto hers. She strained closer, and the ridge of his erection prodded her stomach as he sucked gently on her bottom lip. His fingers stroked her bare hip, across her belly, and then down to the slippery warmth between her thighs. Her clit swelled and ached with the need for him. She moaned against his warm mouth, widening her stance and tightening her arms around his neck.

When his pants and boxers fell around his ankles, he stepped out of them and lifted her against the wall. They came together with urgency, and her internal muscles clamped around him. Still, it felt as if they couldn't get close enough.

"Legs around my waist," Cyrus rasped, hoisting her higher.

She obeyed, and a wild, pulsing dance of their bodies began. Grinding and thrusting, their kisses landed with ravenous intensity.

He thrust deep, hot and hard, and she cried out, burying her face in his neck as pleasure filtered through her veins.

I love you, she thought. The pressure of forthcoming tears burned the back of her eyes, and she squeezed her eyes tight to hold them at bay.

She pressed affectionate kisses to his ear, his neck, and his hard jaw. They mingled with breathless pants against his skin.

He groaned, his big hands on her bottom tightening as he maintained the manic pace. Then, as her body splintered around his, she heard him whisper, "Dani," right before he shook from the force of his own climax.

****

Daniella awoke and listened. By his steady breathing she could tell Cyrus was fast asleep. Easing from his arms, she moved slowly and quietly so as not to wake him. She stood for a while beside the bed and listened to make sure he stayed asleep. When she was certain, she picked up her purse and went into the bathroom. She removed the pack of birth control pills and was about to take one when she noticed she'd miscounted. She paused, studying the packet.

There was an extra one in there, which meant somehow she'd skipped a day. With the time change, she'd lost track and missed one. Or had it been a subconscious decision?

She snapped the container shut. There was no reason for her to continue taking the pills. They were getting along so well, why delay having a child when they both wanted one? She smiled a tremulous smile at the bathroom mirror, acknowledging that yes, she wanted to start a family with him. She loved him, and even though she couldn't tell if he loved her or not, she knew he cared for her, and it was obvious he was trying to make up for the past.

The prospect of having his child no longer seemed daunting. It would be okay. *They* would be okay.

Daniella dropped the pills back into her purse and turned out the light. She climbed into bed, but this time she woke Cyrus when she settled down.

"Why are you all the way over there and I'm all the way over here?" he mumbled drowsily. She smiled. There was barely two inches of space between them.

He pulled her closer and she settled her back against his chest. He kissed the top of her spine, provoking a flicker of desire in her loins. When his hand cupped her breast and started to knead, her desire escalated into a full-on bonfire. She rubbed her ass against his rigid erection, and he groaned.

"Minx," he muttered, grabbing her hips.

He sucked her neck and kneed her legs apart. Throwing her head back, she let out a whimpering moan. He filled her and she gave her body over to the sensations only he could create. She thrust back harder, her heart aching for this temporary connection.

He increased the tempo, almost outpacing her, but she kept time with him. With half her face in the pillow, her lusty cries were muffled and breathless. Her orgasm broke free, and at the same time she felt him stiffen above her.

"Dani," he said, his voice a helpless, broken pant. His entire frame shuddered through the release.

Spent, he kept his weight from collapsing on top of her by bracing himself on his elbows. His warm breath fanned the back of her neck, where damp tendrils clung to her skin. She didn't move and allowed his breathing to return to normal.

He dropped a tender kiss to her shoulder blade. "Missed you so damn much," he said, his voice thick.

She'd missed him, too and had purposely requested they only communicate through their lawyers because to see him or talk to him on a regular basis would have been too hard. Her feelings for him and her decision to leave had warred inside of her for a long time, and now she realized what a mistake she'd made when she left him. She'd been so afraid of losing herself to his dominating personality and afraid of the hurt she'd been sure would eventually come.

Daniella twisted onto her back. She hated the loss of intimate contact with him, but she had to look him in the eye. In the dark, her eyes were adjusted enough to see his proud, angular face. A thin layer of perspiration dotted his forehead and made his dark brown skin shine in the ambient light. "I missed you, too. I won't leave again."

Cyrus dropped his head to her chest and breathed what sounded like a sigh of relief.

CHAPTER SEVENTEEN

For the next two days, Cyrus and Daniella spent their time as tourists. They met the O'Ryans for dinner once—this time managing to actually complete a meal—but the rest of the time they spent alone, exploring the coast.

Today they had rented a car, and with maps in hand they drove to the neighboring town of Mijas Pueblo. In the quaint hillside village, all the buildings and houses were white, and they stopped several times so Daniella could take photos from several vantage points along the way.

Once in Mijas, they visited La Ermita de la Virgen de la Peña, where the virgin was said to have miraculously appeared. The small shrine, formerly a cave, had been excavated in the rocks at the base of the hill that led up to the village. Another must-see was the Plaza de Toros, a small bullring built in 1900 where bull fights were still conducted.

At one of the restaurants in the village they ate a leisurely lunch and then strolled through the streets, stopping every now and again in a shop so Daniella could purchase souvenirs in the form of crafts and leather goods for herself and as gifts.

Before they left, she convinced Cyrus to take a ride on one of the *burro* taxis. Each donkey was covered in beautifully woven fabrics that riders could sit atop, and they were "parked" on the street level near the main plaza. At first Cyrus had been adamant he wouldn't ride one, but she finally talked him into it and giggled at the sight of his tall figure on the small donkey.

"Don't you dare take a photo," he warned.

"Too late." She grinned and snapped another, and they formed a procession with other riders to make their trip to other parts of the village.

By the time they made it back to the car, it was starting to get dark, and they had a long drive back to Málaga.

"I smell like donkey," Cyrus grumbled, sliding into the driver's seat.

"No you don't." Daniella giggled, snapping her seatbelt into place.

He paused with the key in the ignition.

She stopped laughing. "What?"

He reached out and tucked her hair behind her ear. "You're laughing." He said it as if he'd noticed for the first time.

"I've been laughing a lot lately," she said softly. "I guess I'm happy."

He leaned across the seat and kissed her. His mouth was soft and sweet and warm. "Good."

****

"Who are all these things for?" Cyrus asked. They dropped all the bags on the plush settee in the sitting area of their bedroom.

"Friends, my employees, and remember the colorful glass bowls I picked up in the shop with all the ceramics? They would be nice on the shelves in the kitchen, don't you think?" He watched as she took out her earrings and kicked off her shoes, and he couldn't care less about bowls in the kitchen. If she wanted to put them in the bedroom, he'd be fine with that, too.

He stalked over to her and placed his hands on her hips. She tilted her head up to him and graced him with one of her cute smiles. "Did you hear me?" she asked.

"I was distracted by you getting undressed."

"I said, I'm going to take a shower before dinner. Are you planning to join me?"

"Is that a rhetorical question?"

"Silly me." She took a few steps back and pulled the sleeveless top over her head. The satin bra she wore underneath cupped her breasts, and soon he'd be replacing it with his hands. Her lashes lowered over her copper-colored eyes, but couldn't hide the heat in them. "Are you coming?" She turned and added an extra sway to her hips as she headed toward the bedroom, her hand resting provocatively on the zipper at the back of her skirt.

"About to make you come," Cyrus said. He was about to follow when his private cell phone rang. He swore angrily. Since not many people had that number, it had to be important.

"Don't move," he said.

Daniella stayed put at the door, and he looked at the phone. Trenton. Damn.

"Trenton, this better be damn important," Cyrus said into the phone.

"I hate to bother you, but I thought you should know about the latest with Hardy Malcomb."

"Hold on." Cyrus hit the mute button. "I've got to take this," he said to Daniella with regret.

"I'll take my time. Maybe you can catch up and help me finish," she said with a saucy smile. Then she went into the bathroom and closed the door.

She was so good about his work schedule, and he was grateful. Hopefully, he could wrap this up right away and get back to her. The past few days had exceeded his expectations, but they only had a few days left before they had to leave and go back to the States—which he didn't look forward to. He would have preferred to stay longer.

Cyrus unmuted the call. "What's the problem now?" If Hardy had missed the quota again he was going to fire him. Clearly it was time for some new blood because the man had lost his ability to problem solve.

"Seems the hops Hardy claims were bad were actually good enough for him to sell to someone else. He's got his own side deals working."

"*What?*" Cyrus hadn't expected to receive this kind of information. "He's stealing from us? Do you have proof?"

"No, but one of our production managers reported him, and she wants to talk to you directly. You have something to write with?"

Cyrus's eyes swept the room until he spotted Daniella's Chanel bag peeking out from under the plastic and paper sacks filled with souvenirs. She had to have a pen in there. The bag was the size of a small suitcase and he'd once seen her pull out a pair of scissors. "Hold on."

He dug in the front pocket of the purse and didn't find one, so he unzipped the main compartment and rummaged inside. He pulled out a pen, but in his haste knocked the purse to the floor, spilling the contents. Not wanting to keep Trenton holding any longer, he decided to clean up the mess after he'd gotten the details from his brother. Over at the desk he found a notepad and wrote down the name and phone number of the production manager.

"I told her you were on vacation, and she said she could wait until you returned to give you the details."

"What do you think?" Cyrus trusted his brother's judgment.

"I agree, it can wait. A few more days won't make much difference, but I wanted to give you the option in case you thought it was worth pursuing right away. Since you're already in Europe, you may want to even go up to London."

Cyrus stood silently in deep thought. He'd made Daniella a promise and he intended to keep it, which meant he would not cut his trip short for business. He would simply monitor the situation from here. "You're right, it's not an emergency, but keep me up-to-date on what's going on, and I'll speak to…" He glanced down at the paper to get the name right. "Ms. Wozniak in person. Let her know I'll call her in a couple of days to set up a meeting. I'll fly up there before coming back to the States. Until then, let's see if we can give Hardy even more rope to hang himself. Here's what I want you to do." He laid out a plan to work with Ms. Wozniak and how he wanted Trenton to monitor Hardy's actions until he could dig more deeply into the situation. After a few more minutes of conversation, they hung up.

Cyrus felt good about the solution he'd come up with. Still in deep thought about the alleged thefts, he crossed the room, intent on picking up the spilled items from Daniella's purse, when he pulled up short.

Nestled among the usual items of a pack of mints, a cell phone, makeup and a comb, was a small, pink, plastic container.

He hesitated, dread souring his stomach. He recognized the pack for what it was.

Daniella was taking birth control.

He tossed all the items back into her purse and took the pills over to a high-backed chair. Seated on the plush upholstery, he flicked open the container to see half the pills were gone. He fell back in the chair. The shaft of pain that hit his chest couldn't have been more devastating if someone had kicked him in the sternum.

He thought they'd been trying to get pregnant, but she had been on The Pill all along. Lying to him. Deceiving him.

He heard the shower running, but he no longer had any desire to join her. Was she humming? Cold calm came over him and froze his heart. He stayed that way, clutching the contraceptive in his hand, in an almost catatonic state until she exited the bathroom.

She stepped out, wrapped in a large white towel and smelling sweet and fresh. She'd already removed the shower cap, but damp tendrils curled around her face where water had managed to get past the plastic barrier.

"I have an idea," she said, walking over to him, hands on her hips. "I liked where we ate last night, but how about we stay here and order in tonight? What do you think?"

He assessed her smiling face. A fake smile. His chest burned, and his fingers tightened around the plastic container in his hand. He stood. She finally paid attention and noted he wasn't in as good a mood as he had been earlier.

"What's wrong?"

He opened his hand and thrust the container toward her. "What is this?" he asked.

Lines of confusion creased her forehead. "Where did you—"

"What is this?" he asked again. The anger was building. He moved toward her.

She stepped back, away from him and closer to the open bathroom door. "I can explain," she said in a small voice.

"*What. Is. This?*" The words left his mouth as a vicious snarl, a sound coming from his voice box he'd never heard before. He didn't know what she saw in his face, but panic flared in her eyes and she bolted for the bathroom. He followed, but she slammed the door and he heard the lock twist into place.

"Open the door and face me," he said. He pounded twice with his fist, needing to hit something. Needing to break *something*.

"Cyrus, you need to calm down," she said, her voice quivering. "You're not thinking straight."

"Open the door and get out here, Dani. Open this goddamn door now or so help me I'll break it down!"

Her non-response only infuriated him more. Still clutching the pills, the smooth edge of the container cutting into his clenched fingers, he lifted his foot and slammed the heel of his shoe into the wood below the doorknob. The frame splintered and broke apart, and the door swung open and crashed against the inside wall.

Daniella stood in the middle of the opulent bathroom, staring at him with widened eyes. She backed up, hovering in the corner between the counter and shower stall. She thought he'd hurt her, and he wanted to. He'd never experienced this level of anger before. This level of disappointment. This level of *pain*.

"Get out here," he said.

CHAPTER EIGHTEEN

Daniella couldn't say for sure Cyrus wouldn't hurt her. Before tonight, if she'd been asked, she would have given a definitive "no." But the look in his eyes made her confidence waver. She'd never seen such furor, and her heart beat fast in preparation to act quickly.

"No," she said, refusing to leave the bathroom as he'd insisted.

He walked toward her, and she frantically searched for a weapon against him, but all she saw were lotions, a comb, and a brush. All ineffective. She was completely vulnerable against him. He was bigger, stronger, and with the violent emotions coursing through him, much more dangerous.

Cyrus thrust the pills in her face, and she flinched from the sudden movement.

"Tell me you're not taking these," he said.

"I…I had been, but not anymore."

"You had been?" he seethed. He grabbed her by the arm, his fingers as tight as clamps. He brought his face closer to hers. "When exactly did you stop?"

She swallowed. "A few days ago. I swear."

"Really?" He laughed, a mirthless, hollow sound of disbelief. "Isn't that convenient."

"It's the truth. I stopped taking them because we've been getting along and we're so much closer. I didn't see the point anymore."

"So you deceived me," he growled. "You led me to believe you wanted to start a family, when all along you were on The Pill—giving me your body and lying to me with your lips."

"I needed a little time to…to get used to the idea, that's all. I didn't want to bring a baby into this marriage if we weren't going to stay together. You wouldn't give me a choice, so I…I did something I shouldn't have. I admit it, but I've changed, Cyrus, I swear. Please, you have to believe me." Her entreaty fell from lips that trembled with the fear that all was lost.

His eyes glinted down at her, as cold and hard as marbles. "You made a fool out of me. You, the one person…I *trusted* you."

He still hadn't let her go, and she didn't dare try to tug away. "You can trust me. I just made a mistake."

"No, Dani. I was the one who made the mistake of thinking I could trust you to keep your word." He let her go and tore the foil piece containing the pills from the packet. He ripped it into four pieces. He tossed the fragments into the toilet and flushed.

He looked at her, and she waited for him to speak, unable to read his expression because she'd never seen such a look on his face. Her heart was racing, and her arm had gone numb where he'd gripped her. She was numb.

"Cyrus…" she said, breaking the silence. She ached to reach for him, but the look of disgust on his face held her back.

"You win," he said.

She shook her head vehemently. "I wasn't trying to win anything. I don't want to win."

He walked out and she followed.

"Where are you going?" He kept walking, and she kept following. Out the door and down the staircase. "Answer me. Where are you going? What are you doing? Don't leave. Let's talk about this. Please."

Her voice broke at the end, and a braid of fear knotted in her stomach.

"Cyrus, *please*. Don't go."

He ignored her and slammed the door on his way out. She hurried to the window in time to see the motion lights come on. He couldn't get far on foot in the dark. Clearly he just needed to walk off his anger.

She pressed her palms and face to the cool glass. For the most part, he looked the same, but there was one notable difference. His shoulders, normally straight and square, were no longer so.

She closed her eyes and came to the sudden realization of what the unfamiliar expression on his face had been.

Pain.

And she was the cause of it.

****

Daniella waited for him into the late hours of the night, but Cyrus didn't return, and when she called his phone, he didn't answer. Restlessly, she channel-surfed, seeking distractions that failed to get her mind from the problem at hand. Every sound had her hitting mute on the remote and sitting upright in bed, ears cocked for the sound of his footsteps. But each time it was a false alarm.

Finally, in the wee hours of the morning, she was awakened suddenly by his presence in the room. He stood beside the bed, looking down at her. His silence unnerved her.

She sat up. "I know I shouldn't have taken the pills," she started in a rush to explain, "but I changed my mind. I swear to you, I'm not taking them anymore. I want a baby with you. I want a family, like you do."

"Do you?" he asked. He sounded as if he didn't believe her.

"Yes."

"I don't believe a word coming out of that beautiful mouth of yours."

When he yanked the covers off her body, it was completely

unexpected. Her underwear was disposed of quickly, dragged down her legs and tossed aside. He fell on top of her, his mouth fastening onto one covered nipple. The suction of his lips made her pulse between her legs. His teeth raked her cheek, neck, and jawline. He wasn't gentle, but his rough touch didn't keep her from getting aroused.

"Cyrus," she whispered. She ran a hand across his broad back and up to his neck. She turned her head, seeking his mouth, but he twisted away from her.

The unforeseen rejection cut deep, and she felt the pain of it dart through her chest.

He fumbled with his belt, and she lifted her mouth to his again, but again he refused her.

"No," she said in a broken whisper. Desperate, panicked, she grasped his head in her hands and achieved a kiss to the corner of his mouth as he once again denied her the affection.

"No, no." Tears sprang to her eyes. "Cyrus."

They wrestled, she trying in vain to plant a kiss on his mouth, he adeptly avoiding it by pinning her beneath him. She couldn't break free.

She writhed beneath him, refusing to give up. He had to kiss her. He loved kissing her. He'd said so himself.

He forced her onto her stomach and she gasped at the abrupt movement. He pushed her nightgown halfway up her back to expose her bare bottom.

Her throat and eyes filled with tears. "Don't treat me like this," she choked out. She couldn't be sure he understood because the pillow muffled her words.

She wished he was drunk. At least then she could blame his behavior on the alcohol. But he was sober and knew exactly what he was doing.

"Cyrus, please," she begged.

She heard the slide of his zipper and a low grunt as he pulled free of his boxers. She twisted again, struggling against the weight of him on her back. In response, he circled both of her wrists in one hand. His fingers were like steel manacles she couldn't break free of. He kept her pinned down.

"Don't treat me like this," she cried again. The tears flowed freely now. He paused. Whether it was the tears or he finally understood the words, she didn't know. She had his attention. "I'm your wife. I want you to kiss me. *Kiss me.*"

He lowered his lips to her right ear. "You are *not* my wife." The crushing words were a slap in the face. They were brutal. A way to let her know how little she meant to him now.

He slid between the folds of her sex. Slick with want, her body swallowed his wide girth. With one hand clasping her hip and the other holding her wrists together, he pushed all the way in, his hard chest bearing down on her back. Wet and trembling beneath him, she bit her lip and thrust back, arching and clenching her lower muscles to increase the friction and pleasure for them both.

Cyrus increased his speed, his breathing growing shallow.

Her own breaths left her lips in choppy, broken huffs. The tender flesh between her legs opened for deeper penetration, her body not knowing the difference between cold indifference and warm possession, knowing only it was him who touched and filled her to capacity.

Behind her, Cyrus grunted. He was about to come, and he wasn't waiting for her. He'd always seen to her satisfaction first, but not this time.

"Here's another way for us to keep you from suffering through the distasteful burden of having to carry my child," he said. "One you enjoy."

With that, he pulled out, and warm liquid spilled onto her ass. How many times had they done the same thing? Only this time it was different.

Their idyllic vacation, their do-over, was no more. It was over. Her chest contracted painfully tight at the extent of her loss. Still she couldn't let go, couldn't accept it was the end.

Say my name. Please. He always said her name.

Nothing. No more words came from him.

His heavy breathing subsided, and he rested his forehead between her shoulder blades. It was oddly comforting, as if he still wanted to be close to her. At least that's what she chose to believe.

"Cyrus…?" He didn't respond, and what could she say? How could she explain her fears? Her perfectly legitimate reasons for doing what she'd done? He wouldn't believe her anyway.

"Was any of it real?" he asked hoarsely.

Fresh tears burned her eyes. "Yes," she responded in a thick voice.

Whether he heard her or not, she couldn't tell. One second he was behind her, the next he rose from the bed and walked out. She remained in the same position, her wrists crossed and locked together, as if he still held her captive.

The tears came down like a torrential rain. They flowed from her eyes, soaking her cheeks, soaking the pillow. She cried until her eyes were swollen almost shut, and even then she didn't stop.

CHAPTER NINETEEN

Daniella slept badly. In fact, she didn't sleep much at all. Difficult to do, despite the long day and the exhaustive tears she'd cried. She woke up constantly, reliving the nightmare of her night with Cyrus.

Not normally a light sleeper, every sound jerked her awake. One time she thought she heard his footsteps as he entered the bedroom. Then she thought she heard the door open and close. She thought the mattress depressed with the weight of his body as he joined her in bed. Over and over again she would startle awake and then drift into a troubled sleep, only to be awakened again minutes later by more wishful thinking.

The rays of the sun finally forced her from the confines of the bed. She'd much rather stay there, but she had to be up and alert for when he returned. In the bathroom, she stared at her image, appalled at her appearance. Her hair was a tangled mess and her eyes were red and swollen from her constant crying. She fixed her hair but only time could make her face more presentable. She did what she could with makeup.

She didn't leave the house, worried he would come while she was out, so her breakfast was half of a banana because in all honesty she couldn't eat anything more. The minutes dragged by as she waited for him to return or call.

By mid-afternoon she began to worry and called his phone, but there was no answer. They had to talk. She needed to explain. She called five times but he never once picked up. The pain in her chest swelled to an even greater size and she broke down into tears again. Where could he be?

That question was answered when his assistant, Shaun, arrived. It was then she had to accept the gravity of the situation. Cyrus wasn't coming back.

Shaun looked rumpled but alert and ready to work. Cyrus must have called him overnight and told him to come. Downstairs in the entryway, with the sun streaming through the windows, it seemed unbelievable that her marriage had collapsed the night before. The day was bright and pretty—just another day in paradise.

Shaun shoved his glasses up on his nose. Slender but muscular, he had the body of a long distance runner. "I'm here to help you get organized, packed, and back to the States when you're ready," he said. In the past, he'd been pleasant enough, and Daniella didn't know if it was her guilty conscience, but now he seemed standoffish and his blue eyes filled with accusation.

"Where is he?" she asked, uncaring about how Shaun felt about her, uncaring that having to ask such a question should have been embarrassing. She was past embarrassment.

"I'm not sure." His eyes lowered to the ever-present smartphone in his hand. "He told me—"

"Where is he, Shaun?" She wasn't in the mood for avoidance tactics. His allegiance may be to Cyrus, but she needed answers. Cyrus hadn't answered his private phone, the one he always answered, and she knew he had it with him because she'd searched for it and found it missing among the possessions left at the house. "You know his schedule better than anyone else. He tells you everything." There was a slight catch to her voice, and she could tell he heard it.

"He's in London," he finally replied quietly. The look he sent her was a mixture of pity and contrition, as if having to deliver the bad news made him guilty in some way.

Her heart sank. "What's he doing in London?"

"A business emergency came up and he had to fly out immediately." He couldn't even look her in the eye when he lied.

Daniella tempered her tone. It wasn't his fault. He was doing what he'd been told. "You and I both know there was no business emergency."

Shaun remained silent, shifting from his left foot to his right in a display of discomfort.

"I want to go to London to see him."

"That's not a good idea, ma'am. He's working and made it clear what my responsibility was where you are concerned."

If she didn't go with him, he might hog tie her and take her back anyway. Cyrus had given him a directive and he was clearly determined to carry it out.

"So you're here to take me back to Seattle?" Cyrus might be angry at her, but he still made sure she was well-taken care of.

"Yes, ma'am. When would you like to leave?"

"Tomorrow." There was no reason for her to remain there. "When will he be back home?"

"He'll be in London for about a week."

Daniella sighed internally. There were probably legitimate reasons for him to be in London, but she knew urgent business hadn't taken him there. Urgency to get away from her had.

"Thank you, Shaun."

Daniella headed toward the front door. Before she left, she wanted to sit out on the beach and watch the sun bathe the landscape in a burst of bright color before it disappeared.

"Ma'am, he mentioned something about a door...?"

"The bathroom door. It's in the main bedroom. Up the stairs and to the right."

"Thank you." He hurried up the stairs.

"Shaun?" He paused, already halfway up to view the problem and assess how to handle it. "When you talk to him, would you…tell him to call me? Please."

He nodded, the expression of pity and contrition making another appearance. Then he continued up the stairs, and Daniella walked out the door to take one last look at paradise.

CHAPTER TWENTY

Daniella sat impatiently at Seattle Trust Bank. Since her return to the States, she'd charged forward with her plan to get financing to open the gallery in New York. She hadn't heard from Cyrus, although she knew he'd returned a few days ago.

Shaun had shown up at the house to get some of his things and let it slip Cyrus was staying at the Four Seasons Hotel. She'd been tempted to call but didn't know if a longer cooling off period was necessary. Rather than wallow in indecision, she'd continued working on her expansion. With the property under contract, she needed a larger line of credit to purchase inventory and renovate the space, all of which distracted her from her marital problems.

She'd successfully applied for and received a line of credit from the bank almost two years ago, which had allowed her to expand the Ballard location. She'd actually been surprised by the amount they'd loaned her, considering her business had been so young. Her situation had changed drastically since then. Beaux-Arts Galleries had proven itself when she'd made her payments on time, so she saw no reason why she shouldn't get an expansion in her line of credit.

Still, she was nervous. Her banker, Alex, was on vacation and another banker, Bridgette, had come out to greet her and escort her into her office. She was a chunky blonde who smiled when she spoke. Daniella had never seen her before, and it was obvious she was fairly new because she didn't have the same level of confidence Alex did. After accessing Daniella's account via computer, she twisted her hands on the desk, and the nervous action made Daniella uneasy. She didn't know if Bridgette was intimidated or if she was hiding something. In her gut, she felt it was the latter, and she worried it had to do with her husband. She would be sick if he'd influenced the bank into refusing her loan.

"I'm sorry, but we're unable to process your request at this time," Bridgette explained. "Without Alex here, there's not much I can do. He's familiar with your account. Can I provide some other assistance?" She appeared deeply apologetic.

Daniella could feel her fear mounting. They were giving her the brush off. "Surely there's someone else here who can help me. Alex's supervisor, perhaps?" What could possibly be wrong? If they were going to decline her loan request, they needed to let her know.

"Um…I…" Bridgette searched the bank lobby for someone. "One moment, please," she said, and rushed off.

Now Daniella was even more concerned.

Her phone vibrated and she looked down to see a text from her office manager asking how everything was going. She ignored it for now. She didn't have an answer yet.

"Ms. Barrett, I'm so sorry for the delay." Her head lifted at the sound of a man's voice. She recognized him as the bank manager. He wore a suit and had an affable round face. He laughed, an uneasy sound that suggested that they'd screwed up somehow. "We've had this all cleared up. Bridgette is new here and didn't realize we should not keep you waiting. Whatever you need is not a problem."

Daniella blinked, surprised at the turnabout. "Oh. Well, you don't know how much I need."

"How much do you need?" he asked in a cheerful voice. He

clasped his hands in front of him.

"I need another five hundred thousand dollars to do some renovations and purchase inventory for my new gallery in New York. I have the business plan right here." She held it up, but he didn't take it. "I realize I'm asking for a lot of money, but—"

"Absolutely you can!" He laughed heartily and waved his hand as if she was being foolish to suggest otherwise. He didn't even acknowledge the plan she held out to him. "Why don't we make it an even one million?"

Taken aback, Daniella stared at him. "Excuse me?"

"Just in case. Your business is thriving, growing fast, and we don't want you to have to be in this situation again where you need to wait. That will not do. Business decisions need to be made in a split second." He snapped his fingers. "No time for delays."

At a loss for words, Daniella could only look at the man. He was being beyond accommodating by offering twice the requested amount. Had he lost his mind? "I suppose," she said cautiously.

"Wonderful. Stay right there, and we'll type up the paperwork and bring it for you to sign."

"Okay…thank you."

Bridgette brought her water to drink while she waited. Daniella was so stunned she almost forgot to reply to the text and let her employee know the increased line of credit was a go.

Squeeee!! her office manager texted back.

She smiled and texted her back. *LOL. Yes, squee!* Finally, a bit of good news in the mess her life had become.

I'll get started on our plans. So excited!!!

A few days ago, her office manager had suggested they have a party to celebrate the move to New York once the lease had been signed. She suggested sending out invitations to the customers on their mailing list and having a big bash. Even though her heart wasn't in it, Daniella knew she'd have to put on her happy face and go along with the party because it was a good idea. It would allow them to get the word out and plug the New York location at the same time they indulged in a bit of celebration at their success. And her staff deserved this moment to celebrate because they'd worked hard right along with her.

A short time later, Bridgette ushered Daniella into her office to sign the documents for the expanded line of credit. "Thank you so much. I appreciate it," she said, as she scribbled her signature on the appropriate lines.

"It's no problem, of course," Bridgette said. She took the completed paperwork and tapped the ends on the desk. "I'll make a copy for you. Did you need a set for your husband, too?"

Daniella frowned, surprised by the question. "Why would my husband need a set of the documents?"

"I'm sorry. That's a silly question." Bridgette walked around the desk. "I assumed since Mr. Johnson guaranteed the line of credit, he would get a copy."

"Since…wait a minute, *what?*" Daniella stood up, effectively halting Bridgette on her way out the door. "What do you mean my husband guaranteed the line of credit? He has nothing to do with Beaux-Arts Galleries."

Bridgette's lips formed into a perfect circle of dismay. Two spots the same color as her red lipstick flamed her cheeks in rouge. "I—I'm sorry. Perhaps I misspoke." She swallowed.

"No, you didn't. What does my husband, Cyrus Johnson, have to do with this?"

"I'm s-sorry, Ms. Barrett. Please…" Bridgette looked helplessly at the open door, seeking to escape but knowing she couldn't bolt in the middle of the conversation.

"I want an answer," Daniella said. Her voice had grown louder, and a patron seated outside the door looked up from the magazine in his hands.

The bank manager appeared in the doorway. "Is there a problem?" He looked from one to the other.

"I…I said something I guess I shouldn't have," Bridgette stuttered. At this point, her entire face had reddened. When she explained what she'd done, the blood drained from the manager's face.

"Did you give me that money because of who my husband is?" Daniella asked.

He lifted a placating hand to her. "Ms. Barrett, please, you have to understand…please don't tell your husband. He told us not to say anything, and Bridgette didn't know."

Beside him, Bridgette's head bounced up and down in agreement.

"Are you saying Cyrus knows about this? Did you call him and tell him I asked for an expanded line of credit?" If so, it was an astronomical breach of confidentiality.

"No. But Mr. Johnson handpicked Alex to handle your affairs and insisted you receive whatever you need whenever you requested it."

"That's impossible," Daniella said. "The first loan you gave me was almost two years ago." She'd already filed for divorce by then.

"That's correct, ma'am, and the agreement has been in place ever since. Then, approximately two months ago, your husband contacted us to confirm it was still intact. We assured him it was."

Daniella knew what would have prompted him to call. The night of Ivy's engagement party, when she'd told him about her plan to expand to New York. He'd taken the information from the casual question he'd asked about her business to reaffirm the safety net he'd put in place for her was still intact. He didn't want anything standing in the way of her expansion plans.

"We've been doing business with the Johnson family for years," the manager continued. "We would never go against his instructions."

"I don't understand. Why would he do that?" Daniella wondered out loud. She'd meant it to be a rhetorical question, but Bridgette answered.

"Why wouldn't he?" she asked, confusion etched in her face. "He's your husband."

True, he was her husband, even though he no longer wanted to be. The extent to which he'd gone to ensure her success boggled her mind.

They waited for her response, and she realized that because of who she was, who she had married, they were extremely nervous and worried about the outcome of today's visit. If she complained to Cyrus, they were concerned he'd be so annoyed he'd move his money to a different bank because his explicit instructions had not been followed. While she knew he and his family did business with other banks—spreading the risk, he would call it—to be able to say this was one of them was quite an honor. It spoke volumes that the Johnsons entrusted Seattle Trust Bank with their financial assets and had done so for years.

"I won't say anything to my husband," she assured them.

"Oh, thank God," the manager blurted, slumping against the wall. Then, as if he realized he'd said it out loud, he blushed and straightened. "I mean, thank you. We'll get you taken care of right away," he said.

"Right away," Bridgette echoed.

They rushed from the office, and Daniella retook her seat, overwhelmed by what she had learned. She stared down at the rings on her finger. Her heart was heavy.

What was Cyrus doing now? Did he think about her as much as she thought about him? Did he still want to make her happy, or had she killed all of the affection he'd held for her? What else had he done that went unnoticed and unappreciated? Yet he kept on working, kept on doing—unselfishly, expecting nothing in return, and all without a word of thanks.

****

With loan documents in hand, Daniella exited the bank. She

should have been ecstatic, but her mood was tempered by what she'd come to accept about her husband. She was so distracted by her thoughts that she didn't see Roland on the sidewalk.

"Hey." He put up his hands and stopped her. "How are you? Are you okay?"

The last time they'd spoken was when she'd called to tell him Cyrus would give him his job back. To be honest, she wasn't in the mood to talk to him now. "I'm fine. I have a lot on my mind."

"I know we haven't talked, but um…after Cyrus gave me my job back, he sold his interest in BoldMine to a group of investors specializing in technology companies."

"Congratulations. I should probably go…"

His hand on her arm detained her. "Would you like to grab a coffee or something?"

"I don't think that's a good idea," Daniella said with a shake of her head. "You know how Cyrus feels about you and me being together."

"So you're going to do whatever your husband says?" Roland laughed.

"I don't do *whatever* he says, but—"

"Not you, too, Daniella. You used to have your own mind. Tell me you're not like everybody else, falling all over yourself and drinking the Johnson Kool-Aid."

His comments stung. "*I'm* a Johnson." She may not have been born into the family, but she was part of them now. After they'd separated she dropped that part of her name, but now she finally accepted it, and she wouldn't tolerate Roland or anyone else making disparaging remarks about them.

Roland looked taken aback, his eyebrows elevating over his eyes. "What's happened to you? You're still trying to get a divorce, aren't you? You know Cyrus is a control freak who uses questionable methods to get what he wants. Look at what he did to me."

"What he did to you? You took the money he offered and then ratted him out. So what does that say about you?" Roland had clearly forgotten his role in the matter.

"I was desperate, but I think I proved how much I cared about you when I tracked you down and apologized."

"That had nothing to do with caring about me," Daniella said. She'd thought long and hard about his reappearance in her life and recognized the truth. "You thought your company was about to take off, and you wanted to get back at Cyrus through me. He forced you to see your true self—someone who would do anything for money. You hated him for it, and maybe you even hated me a little bit because I married him after you and I broke up."

"That's a ridiculous theory."

"Is it?"

His eyes hardened. "You're not going to leave him, are you? Being married to him has finally turned you into a Johnson clone."

Daniella's patience snapped in half. "No, being married to him has made me realize what a good man he is. He has more integrity in his little finger than you have in your entire body. He may not be perfect, but he protects the people he loves and he's a man of his word. And that, Roland, is more than I can say about you."

She left him standing on the corner, a look of bewilderment on his face.

She hurried to her car in the parking lot and hopped in. She tossed the bank paperwork on the passenger seat and took a breath to calm down.

What if Cyrus never forgave her? The thought of losing him was unbearable. He *had* to take her back. She wrapped her hand around her waist to calm her queasy stomach.

But if she wanted forgiveness, she had to give it, too. Time to make some changes in her life.

She pulled her cell phone from her purse and dialed 411.

"Welcome to directory assistance. City and state, please," the automated voice said.

Daniella closed her eyes, clutching the phone tight in her hands. "Miami, Florida."

"Say the name of the business you want, or say residence."

"Residence."

An operator came on the line. "Hello. What is the last name of the person you're trying to reach?"

"Barrett." She gripped the steering wheel, needing the support.

"And the first name?"

"Carlos," Daniella whispered. Her throat had drawn so tight she could barely speak.

"Excuse me?"

"Carlos," Daniella said, louder. "The name is Carlos Barrett."

CHAPTER TWENTY-ONE

Daniella knew what she was doing was rotten, but it was the only thing she could think of to salvage her marriage. Davis, her attorney, looked across his crowded desk at her, his bushy gray brows furrowed in concern.

"What are you doing?" he asked. "You're about to be free from your husband—something you've tried to accomplish for three years. Everything you've asked for, he's given you. Then you make another request, which delays the proceedings, and now you want the house?" It wasn't just concern in his voice. He was appalled at her request.

"What's your point?" Daniella asked.

Cyrus had used the courts to delay what he didn't want to happen. Now she was doing the same. Any woman would be happy with such a generous settlement and the newfound ease she had in dissolving her marriage. Cyrus was giving her above and beyond what she'd requested. He'd even offered to pay her attorney fees, but his generosity only reminded her of how much their relationship had disintegrated. How much he wanted her out of his life.

"Your husband's being surprisingly generous. In addition to the settlement he's given you according to the prenup, you're going to receive generous spousal support, much more than I expected. He's not fighting you on anything. All you have to do is sign."

"I want the house," Daniella said, refusing to budge, no matter how ridiculous she sounded. She didn't need the house and certainly couldn't afford it's upkeep. She would save the request for a maintenance allowance, in case she needed it, but didn't think she would. Cyrus would never give up the mansion. Not only did he love the house, he appreciated the privacy of the neighborhood.

Davis's expression turned thoughtful. "If I didn't know better…" He hesitated, but she knew he saw through her ruse, although he hesitated to call her on it. "If you ask for too much, this whole process could fall apart and we'll be back to square one."

That's what she was hoping for. She twisted the rings on her finger. "He'll never give up the house," she said with confidence. "He'll fight me." Which would delay the divorce, which meant she could hold onto him that much longer and he couldn't move on.

"I don't doubt he will. He bought it before you were married, and he's already agreed to give you the flat in London." It had been purchased after they married, but she didn't want it either. He found it more convenient to stay there than at a hotel when he visited Johnson Enterprises European headquarters. She had no use for the place, but Cyrus had been surprisingly amenable to turning it over to her. With regard to the house, though, she was confident he wouldn't budge.

"I decorated the house," she said, knowing that in no way justified her desire to own it. The money for every piece of furniture, painting, and decorative item had come from his bank account. She'd been given carte blanche to make changes as she see fit. "I want the Bentley, too."

Her attorney's mouth fell open. He must think she was a crazy, callous bitch. "Daniella, the chances…"

"I don't care about chances," she said firmly. She stood. "Make the request."

"You understand that if he doesn't give in on what you want, this could drag out for months."

"I understand, but what do you care? He'll cover your fees. Do as I ask, or I'll find another attorney who will." She'd been unnecessarily harsh, but she couldn't afford for him to ruin her plan.

Davis sat up. "I'll have the revisions for you right away."

"Take your time. There's no rush."

She left right after, heading back to the gallery even though it was late in the day. She dreaded going back to the house and facing Ms. Ernestine and the rest of the staff. They couldn't possibly know the details of what had transpired between her and Cyrus, but somehow she felt they did and silently condemned her.

They continued to keep the house in the same orderly fashion he preferred, as if he was still there, but as far as Daniella knew, he hadn't returned once.

She wanted to send a message to Cyrus through Shaun, but after the message he'd relayed through her attorney that they should only communicate through their lawyers, she'd decided against it. She thought about going to his office and confronting him, but she was afraid he might have had her barred from the building. She had a not-so-humorous thought of him sending her photo down to the security guards, similar to a mugshot, and warning she should not be allowed to get past the atrium. Even if she did, she'd never get past Roxanne. The woman was a bulldog when it came to him and wouldn't hesitate to make the call to have her thrown out of the building.

She'd have to wait and continue on the same course. Using the divorce was the only way she could think of to stay in Cyrus's life for now. Until a better idea came along.

****

Cyrus stared down at the dinner plate. Fish, rice pilaf, and vegetables stared back at him. He couldn't even taste the food. He'd lost the taste for a lot of things lately. He'd been working harder than ever in an effort to forget Daniella, but hadn't succeeded in doing so. Once she entered his thoughts, he couldn't expunge her. Not even in sleep could he get any rest. At random times he woke up in the middle of the night and reached for her, only to find the empty space beside him in the bed.

He had to stay focused. People depended on him. His attorney thought he was crazy for not fighting Daniella on any of her requests, but if any part of him was good, he had to correct his past wrongs and do right by her. He had to give her the one thing he'd denied her all along because of his own selfishness. Her freedom.

The sooner the better. Nothing she asked for was irreplaceable, but his attorney disagreed with his decisions. Especially concerning the house.

"She's asking for your house, Cyrus. She has no legitimate claim to it. You lived in it before you married her."

Cyrus shrugged. *"She helped me decorate it. Maybe she's in love with the place. I really don't care."* What was the point of holding onto the property? There were too many memories of Daniella there. All her touches in the colors and the furnishings. He would find another place, something smaller and more practical. For now, the Four Seasons Hotel served his purposes. Maybe he'd buy Ivy's condo since she and Lucas had mentioned they wanted a larger place for after they were married.

"As your attorney, I have to advise you the concessions you're making are not in your best interest."

"I'm fully aware of what my best interests are, but I want to get this over with. These proceedings have gone on long enough, haven't they?"

"Cyrus?"

He looked up into his mother's kind, worried eyes. Around the table, the rest of the family observed him with concern. Trenton, to his left, and across from him Ivy, Lucas, Katie, and Xavier.

"Is the food not to your liking?" his mother asked. "I could have Adelina make something else."

"I'm all right, Mother. I'm just not very hungry."

He sliced into the fish and placed a morsel in his mouth but didn't miss the look that passed between her and Trenton.

"I heard you've changed your schedule a bit." His mother's voice was cautious. It was unusual for her to be so careful. She usually spoke her mind and had the talent so many Southern women possessed—the ability to insult you while smiling, and it was only later you realized you should be offended by their deceptively innocent remark.

"Who told you I changed my schedule?"

"Ivy happened to mention it."

He glanced at his sister. "And what did Ivy say?"

His mother dabbed at the corner of her mouth with the cloth napkin. "She mentioned you've been off your routine. Security said you've been showing up late for work."

Cyrus sat back and looked at his sister. "So you have security keeping tabs on me?"

"No, I don't," Ivy said.

"I'm at work by seven-thirty."

"You have to admit that's later than normal for you. You usually get in earlier and work out."

"What Mother is trying to say," Trenton interrupted, "is that everyone's worried about you because you're not acting like yourself."

They all had their eyes on him, and they were filled with worry. Even his niece, Katie. It was unnerving to see such concern, as if he'd somehow fallen short. The way they were behaving made him feel as if this was an intervention. He was the oldest and his father had charged him with the important task of being the head of the family and taking care of *them*—not the other way around.

"I'm fine," he said shortly. "I have a lot on my mind."

"Do you want to talk about it…privately?" his mother asked quietly.

"No, I don't. As a matter of fact, I should go into the office and get some work done."

The concern in his mother's eyes deepened. "It's Sunday."

Oh yeah, it was.

Since he and Daniella separated for the second time, he had been distracted and zoned out at the oddest times. One day he'd even driven to her gallery. He hadn't realized he was on his way there until he pulled up outside. Since he was there, he thought he'd talk to her, maybe even apologize for his heinous behavior their last night together in Spain.

But he had been ill prepared for the sight of his wife, standing amidst a crowd of smiling faces wishing her well as they toasted the New York location. She'd looked so…*happy*. So content, he hadn't wanted to spoil her special night with his presence. He'd slipped away unnoticed and sat in the car, finally accepting it was indeed over. Even in their happiest moments, he was convinced she'd never looked so radiant.

Love, a pure form of it reserved only for her—had been pushed back down where it belonged. No point in getting his hopes up. No point in thinking that maybe if he had been a different man from the beginning, she could love him.

In a moment of introspection, he knew without a doubt she could never love him. Why would she? He'd never given her a single reason to.

Cyrus scraped his chair back. Sunday dinners were important to his mother, but he couldn't stay there any longer and face the pitying looks of his family members. Hell, maybe he *would* go to work.

"Mother, I'm sorry to disrupt dinner, but I can't do this right now. No need to worry about Johnson Enterprises, though. The business won't suffer."

His mother frowned. "I'm not worried about the business, son. I'm worried about you."

"We've never seen you like this," Trenton added.

"Everything is fine. I'm fine. No need for anyone to worry."

Cyrus kissed his mother on the cheek and saw her look desperately at his brother, Xavier. A message was conveyed, and Xavier rose immediately to his feet. Cyrus didn't stick around. He left the dining room without any intention of talking to his brother.

"Hang on a minute." Xavier caught up to him in the foyer.

Cyrus spun around. "I'm fine," he said through gritted teeth. He glanced at his watch as if he had a pressing appointment.

"I'm sure you are, but that's not why I stopped you."

Cyrus raised an eyebrow in skepticism.

"Well, it is, but before we get to the part about you, I wanted to talk to you about what we discussed at Ivy's engagement party."

"What about it?" Cyrus said impatiently. He wasn't in the mood to argue.

Xavier appeared uncertain, as if unsure of what to say. "Maybe I could...come back and help out with the company."

Cyrus hadn't expected him to say that. "You're actually interested?"

He shrugged. "You could say I am, but what would I do there?"

Cyrus considered his brother for a moment. "What brought this on?"

"Like I said, I've been thinking about what you said."

This was good news. With Xavier working at Johnson Enterprises, they'd all be there except Gavin, and he knew Xavier would do a good job once he'd been fully trained.

"Well, with your background in finance, the logical position would be CFO, but we have one already and I'd much rather have you in a different position. You should become the COO of the company, work closely with me and learn the ropes, the same way I did when Father was alive. There's a corner office sitting empty on the executive floor. All you have to do is put your name on it and move in."

Xavier nodded thoughtfully. "I need to tie up a few things before I bail on the nonprofits. I still want to be involved with them in some capacity. These projects are important to me."

"Understandable, but with our financial resources, you could still work with those organizations and be a voice for change, the way you want."

"Would I have to wear a suit?"

"Yes. I'll get you in touch with my tailor." He looked his brother up and down, taking in the dashiki and distressed jeans. "We can't have you walking around the offices looking like a drugged out Rastafarian. No offense."

A smile softened the corner of Xavier's mouth. "Offense taken."

They grinned at each other. Something they hadn't done in a long time.

"Now, to your personal life…"

Cyrus sighed. "You're all worried about nothing."

"Make up with your wife. I can't stand to see you operating at less than one hundred percent. If you aren't together mentally, the rest of us are screwed."

"Dani and I didn't work out. It's really over this time." He considered himself a strong man, but losing her again had rocked him—hard. His life was not the same and he knew it never would be.

"Damn," Xavier said in a grave voice. "You guys couldn't fix it, huh?"

It was with great effort Cyrus shrugged and downplayed the catastrophe that was his marriage. "No." He didn't meet Xavier's gaze because he didn't want him to see how much the separation from Daniella affected him. During moments alone when he dwelled on their separation, he likened the empty, hollow ache to that of losing a vital organ. "I better go so I can get in to work early enough for security to report to Ivy I'm back on my schedule."

As he was turning away, he heard Katie's soft voice. "Uncle Cyrus." She stood uncertainly in the hallway with her hands behind her back. Concerned brown eyes looked up at him through her glasses. "Are you okay?"

He smiled at his niece. "I'm not at my best right now," he admitted.

"Do you need a hug?" she asked. That was about the best idea he'd heard in a long time.

"Yeah."

Katie rushed over and wrapped her arms around his waist. She squeezed hard and he hugged her back.

"Thank you," he said softly, and kissed the top of her head.

She looked up at him. "I'll call you tomorrow to make sure you're doing fine."

"Thank you, Munchkin."

She and Xavier went back to the dining room, and Cyrus left his mother's house. Unfortunately, he wouldn't feel any better when Katie called him. Reason being, he'd tasted heaven. Now anything else felt like hell.

CHAPTER TWENTY-TWO

Cyrus pulled up in front of the Four Seasons Hotel and stepped out of his car. He handed the keys to the valet. It was almost ten o'clock at night and he'd left work fifteen minutes before. Entering the empty suite he now called home didn't appeal to him, but he couldn't stay at work forever.

Briefcase in hand, he flung his jacket over his shoulder and had strolled halfway through the foyer to the bank of elevators when he saw Daniella walking toward him. His steps slowed, but his heart started racing.

"Hi, Cyrus," she said.

His gaze traveled over her from head to toe. A chocolate pencil skirt fit snug over her hips and a silk blouse in a lighter brown flattered her full bosom. Her long hair hung in loose, ebony waves over her shoulder and down her back. "What are you doing here?" he asked.

"Can I talk to you?" She looked discomforted, as if she was nervous.

"Do you need something?" His eyes searched her face. He would give her whatever she needed. He hoped she at least knew that.

"I need to talk to you," she replied.

"How long have you been waiting here?" he asked.

"Not long. I figured you'd be working late." Her smile was timid. "Do you mind if I come up?"

He almost said no, because he couldn't tolerate having her presence in his new sanctuary. At least there only his thoughts tormented him, but if Daniella came upstairs, he'd have the memory of seeing her in this new space, too.

His own selfish urges won out.

"Sure, you can come up," he said with a curt nod.

Neither of them spoke all the way up to the tenth floor. They stood at opposite ends of the elevator, the way strangers do. At the presidential suite, he opened the door and let her enter first, using the opportunity to assess the way the material of her skirt stretched over her plump little ass. She smelled good, too, and he wanted to lean closer and gratify his senses with the scent of her. The light in the entryway illuminated her hair, giving it the appearance of smooth silk. He wanted to sift his fingers through the lush strands and experience their softness again, but he fought the urge.

In the living room he set down his briefcase and tossed his jacket over the back of the sofa.

She stood awkwardly in the center of the room. "This is nice."

Earth tones dominated the room's decorations, and in the living room, dining room, and bedroom he had great views of Elliott Bay through the floor to ceiling windows.

"It's fine, and big enough to suit my purposes." This was what they'd devolved to—inane pleasantries about his living arrangements. "What did you want to talk to me about?"

"I don't know how to say this." Daniella wrung her hands together. Now that she was here, she was a nervous wreck to tell Cyrus her news. She stared down at her shoes, summoning the courage to say the words she'd practiced all day. She finally looked up at him. "I'm pregnant."

No movement from him, no reaction at all. He stared at her as if he was disoriented. She understood the feeling. She'd been shocked herself when the doctor told her. Once the initial surprise wore off, she'd recognized the opportunity her pregnancy presented. It was a chance to start a family with the man she loved, and an ace in the hole she'd been waiting for to orchestrate a reconciliation between them.

"Did you hear me?" she asked.

His gaze fell to her waistline. Then there was the smallest of movements—a twitch right above his eyebrow before he abruptly turned away as if he could no longer bear to look her. His shoulders became as taut and rigid as wooden planks.

"How far along are you?"

"Ten weeks," she replied, and she could almost see him doing the math to determine the time of conception, the same as she had, when she'd figured out she'd gotten pregnant in Málaga.

He'd have to take her back now. She tossed her hair, fluffing it with her fingers. Wearing her hair down had been a calculated decision because she knew he liked it this way.

The cadence of her heart sped up as she waited, anticipated he would tell her they had to stay married. That he wanted a prominent role in his child's life and they would live together as husband and wife—as a family—to make sure that happened. Their child would be the bridge to bring them back together, the way they were before he found her prescription. He'd had feelings for her. She'd seen it in his face and in his actions.

"Joint custody is the only arrangement I'll accept." Cyrus's voice sounded detached, hollow. "That's nonnegotiable. I'll have my lawyer draw up new papers to include child support."

What? Her heart juddered and then stopped before starting again at an even faster, panicked pace. That wasn't the response she'd expected.

"I'm carrying your baby."

"Which you didn't want in the first place," he said, his voice devoid of emotion and his body still ramrod straight. "I understand, and I want to make this as easy for you as possible, which includes giving you the house, as you requested, and of course enough to maintain it." He continued to stare out of the window into the night.

Why wouldn't he look at her? They should be celebrating right now. Why didn't he grab her and hug her and tell her of his excitement? That all was forgiven and they could start over?

Daniella licked her dry lips, true panic setting in. He was supposed to come back home. "I don't understand. You love that house," she said, hoping she'd effectively hidden the dismay in her voice. Her last chance to hold onto him was slipping away. Why was he giving her all of these *things*?

He turned away from the window and studied her for long seconds before responding. "It's just a house. It's not that important. You'll need it more than I do with the baby coming. This place serves my needs."

For the first time she noticed he wasn't wearing his ring. He'd worn that ring for the three years of their separation. Now it was gone, and the shock of its absence splintered her heart into fragments. He'd officially given up on their marriage.

He didn't even want the house—his beloved house. He would give her anything she wanted to get rid of her.

She drifted back into the conversation, catching the last bit of his current sentence. "…get Shaun to start research on someone to help with the baby."

Eyes on her feet, Daniella nodded numbly, afraid if she tried to speak she'd fall to her knees, grab him about the ankles, and beg him to forgive her.

"So everything is settled?" he asked.

She barely managed to nod again—paralyzed, finding it hard to move.

"Thank you for letting me know. I appreciate you coming to tell me in person." So impersonal, as if he was thanking one of his employees.

Tears burned the back of her throat, but she managed to keep her composure. She could barely see her feet through the cloud of tears.

She couldn't fall apart. Not here. Not now. Not in front of him.

Where was her purse? Daniella scanned the room.

Forget it. She'd leave it. She had to get out. Everything around her was distorted because of the moisture in her eyes. She blinked rapidly and rushed toward the door. A tear crept from the corner of her eye, and she brushed it away.

"Dani?"

His voice halted her escape. She placed a hand to her stomach to smother the pain expanding there. What was he going to give her now? More money? Another car? Another house?

"I can't do this." The words were spoken so low, she almost didn't hear them. His voice sounded strangled. Strained, even. "I can't...I can't let you go. I know it makes me selfish, and I'm an asshole, but you have to give me another chance. I want..." His voice fell off, the heaviness of it calling out to her. She held her breath as she listened. "We'll go on more dates, and we'll take things slow. Real slow. Slower than we did before. I...I can't let you go again, Dani. I'm miserable without you. I need you. I love you. I want us to raise our child together. I can't get through the rest of my life without you."

She finally faced him, her emotions no longer a precarious jumble because he'd said the words she'd longed to hear. Slowly, she moved toward him. Then stopped. "You love me?"

He stood proudly, his handsome face taut with tension, his chin tilted up and body braced like a fighter preparing for a blow. "Yes, and I'm not giving up on us. I refuse to—"

He never finished because she rushed toward him and wrapped her arms around his body, squeezing her eyes shut.

"Dani?" Confusion colored his voice, and she laughed. It was a shaky but contented sound.

"I love you, I love you, I love you," she whispered.

Cradling her face in his hands, he tilted her head up and searched her eyes, clearly unable to believe what he'd heard. The coffee-dark eyes of her big, strong, invincible husband were filled with anxiety, and the frown he wore was so cute.

With her fingertip, she traced the crease in his forehead and made the lines disappear. "I love you, Cyrus, and I don't want to go through life without you, either."

Long seconds ticked slowly by before her words finally registered. A wide grin broke out on his face, like nothing she'd ever seen before. There was no arrogance or smugness, only pure and simple joy. He rested his forehead against hers. "Dani, you're my life. I was so lost without you." He planted a tender kiss on her mouth, and she sighed with happiness.

"I was lost without you, too."

EPILOGUE

Their son arrived in the world with an imperious cry forewarning everyone that even at such a young age he was ready to take over the world. They named him Michael Andrew—giving him the middle name of his father and his grandfather, but his own first name. Family members had been surprised, some even disappointed, expecting a Cyrus the third. But Daniella understood how important it was for her husband to allow their son to have his own identity, and she supported his decision.

The family's PR firm released the name and photos to the press to avoid the mad dash for the first image of the newest member of the Johnson family dynasty.

For his part, Cyrus was as involved as he could be with their son's care. Xavier working at the company allowed him to pass on some of the operations, which freed him to come home a little earlier and significantly cut the time he had to travel for business.

Every free moment he had, he spent with his son, playing and talking to him. A spare playpen had been set up in his home office, with plenty of colorful toys for Michael to occupy himself with. Yet it wasn't unusual to see Cyrus holding his son in one hand and typing with the other. Michael was also captivated with his father. He was especially drawn to his voice. Every time he heard it, he turned in his father's direction and stared, his brown eyes wide and alert, as if soaking up bits of knowledge in every single word.

****

Daniella said goodnight to her father and hung up the phone. She climbed the stairs to the second floor. She and Carlos spoke on a regular basis now, but tonight's conversation had lasted longer than usual.

The upstairs hall was quiet. Outside the nursery door she met the nanny, a buxom black woman they'd hired from England to help with Michael's care.

"He won't let me do my job," the nanny whispered, a frown settling over her features.

They'd discussed the situation before, how whenever Cyrus was around, the nanny seldom had the opportunity to take care of Michael. The woman was worried she would be seen as useless and then dismissed, and Daniella's reassurances hadn't been enough.

"I'll take care of it." She patted the nanny's arm.

"Well…"

"We'll see you in the morning," Daniella said with a smile.

"All right, then." She still appeared uncertain and lingered for a moment before finally taking the stairs down to the lower level.

Daniella entered the nursery to find Cyrus seated in the wing back chair beside the baby's crib. He held four-month-old Michael in one arm, safe and sound against his bare chest, both of them fast asleep. She stood there for a moment, taking private pleasure in watching them both. She'd snapped photos of them like this before, so it was nothing new, but the sight still warmed her insides.

Cyrus was every bit the doting father she'd expected him to be. She couldn't imagine what the employees and business people he dealt with every day would think if they saw him the way he was tonight— in a pair of dark slacks, cradling his son against his chest. He could bottle feed and burp with the best of them. Changing diapers was another matter altogether. Whenever his son soiled his diaper, Cyrus always found her or the nanny, holding his son away from him with a wrinkled nose. It was the only time he would willingly hand him over.

He claimed he was no good at changing diapers. Cyrus Johnson, who did everything perfectly. Yeah, right. She smiled to herself as she watched him. That was his excuse so he wouldn't have to perform the unsavory task.

She placed a hand on his shoulder and whispered his name. His eyes flew open and he blinked several times to catch himself. "Time for you to go to bed."

He had an early meeting before a flight to London the next day. They were still searching for someone to head up European production. A headhunting firm had narrowed down and vetted the list of candidates, and he and Xavier were on their way to London to interview Hardy Malcomb's potential replacements.

She lifted their son out of Cyrus's arms and Michael protested, whimpering until she rocked him back to sleep with soothing caresses to his back. She kissed her little bundle's soft cheek before placing him carefully in the crib. When she turned around she saw Cyrus staring at their son between the slats. He was always staring at their son, as if he still couldn't believe Michael actually existed.

She took his hand. "Come on."

She led him into their bedroom and sat him on the bed. She knelt before him and removed his shoes and socks. When she stood and started unbuckling his belt, he pulled her between his legs, and his hands slipped to her bottom.

"How's your father?" he asked.

"They want us to come visit," she said. Carlos and his wife had moved to the beautiful island of St. John. He had invited her, Cyrus, and Michael to come see them, and she'd promised to discuss it with Cyrus. A year ago she would never have guessed she could have such a fulfilling relationship with her father. The resentment she felt toward his wife was still hard to set aside, but she was working on it.

By reconnecting with her father, she'd learned a few things about his relationship with her mother she hadn't known before. He had, in fact, tried to reestablish a relationship with Daniella after he divorced her mother, but her mother had been opposed to it. He'd overnighted a box of mementos—cards and letters he'd sent her for the first five years after the divorce that had been returned unopened. Afterward, he'd given up.

When she demanded to know why he didn't try harder, he'd said, "*After what I'd done, I felt she needed you more than I did.*"

Her mother's role in her painful past had been difficult to digest, but Daniella had accepted it and forgiven her. People made poor decisions when they loved deeply. She knew all about that.

"I think it's a good idea to go see them," Cyrus said. "I'm sure he's looking forward to seeing his grandson in the flesh."

"He is, so you'll have to let someone else hold Michael for a change."

He chuckled. "I'll consider it."

She kissed his forehead. "You need to go to sleep," she said, pushing away his hands, even though she enjoyed his touch. "You have a big day tomorrow and you've had a crazy weekend."

"I'm still awake," he pointed out, looking down at the rise in his pants.

"Behave." She slapped his roving hand, but he pulled her down on top of him.

"At least turn off the lights," she whispered.

"No way. I want to look at you. I never get tired of looking at you."

Daniella smiled contentedly and rewarded her husband with a deep kiss. She appreciated him so much, and how could she not love him when he constantly reassured her she was still as beautiful and sexy as ever?

She was self-conscious about the weight she hadn't taken off since the baby's arrival, but Cyrus didn't seem to mind at all. It bothered her, though. Maybe because she'd always been thin, but she wanted to get as close to her former weight as possible. She'd recently hired a personal trainer to help her lose those last pounds, and since he was a sadistic drill sergeant, she expected to be back to her old self in no time.

Their lovemaking was an unhurried exploration where his hands brushed across her nipples and moved slowly along the contours of her waist and hips. His mouth trailed over her nakedness in the same leisurely fashion and, as if to reassure her, he kissed her rounded belly and the stretch marks on her hips, which he affectionately called her "tiger stripes."

She welcomed him between her legs with a contented sigh. His hips rocked back and forth—slowly, gently. Moaning and matching his movements, she wrapped her arms around his strong neck as tension tightened in her belly. Gradually, their breathing became sporadic and their words came out like broken beats of heated air. When she climaxed, her entire body gripped his—arms, legs, even teeth, which she sank into his shoulder.

Afterward, he turned out the lights and she lay her head on his shoulder, an arm thrown across his firm stomach. They lay quietly, with him lightly rubbing her bare back, from her shoulder blades down to the curve in her lower spine.

"Michael's getting so big," Cyrus said after a few minutes.

"Babies grow fast," she agreed. She fell silent, but she couldn't sleep. "Are you still awake?" she asked, when he had stopped caressing her back.

"Mhmm."

"Can we get our own place in Costa del Sol? I love it there. Nothing big. Maybe one of those little white houses on the hillside near Mijas, with a rooftop terrace and a little yard. Or even a place on the beach. Something with a few bedrooms. One for us, Michael, and our next one." They'd discussed having at least one more child.

"Sure. I'll get Shaun to do some research and you can decide what you want."

"I want you to choose with me," she said, watching his profile in the darkness.

"Okay, whatever you want." He was slipping fast. She could hear it in his speech.

She pressed her nose to his neck. She loved to smell him. "Thank you. You're such a sweetheart."

He growled. "Stop calling me that. You make it sound like I'm a big softie."

"You are," she teased. "You're *my* big softie. My teddy bear."

"I'm a grizzly bear."

"No matter what you say, you're my teddy bear."

"Grizzly," he countered. Of course he'd have to have the last word.

Daniella kissed his cheek, and within a few minutes he started snoring. To have fallen asleep so fast, he was definitely tired.

She nudged him. "You're snoring," she said.

"Sorry, sweetheart," he mumbled. He shifted in the bed so he lay on his side and pulled her against him so they were spooning. "Better?"

"Mhmm." She snuggled deeper into his arms.

Her life was much better than it had ever been and surpassed her expectations. She'd mended the relationship with her father. She had a husband who loved and supported her. Her business was doing well and her son was healthy and happy. Life couldn't be better.

In a word, it was...perfect.

The End

MORE STORIES BY DELANEY DIAMOND

Hot Latin Men series
The Arrangement
Fight for Love
Private Acts
Second Chances
Hot Latin Men: Vol. I (print anthology)
Hot Latin Men: Vol. II (print anthology)

Hawthorne Family series
The Temptation of a Good Man
A Hard Man to Love
Here Comes Trouble
For Better or Worse
Hawthorne Family Series: Vol. I (print anthology)
Hawthorne Family Series: Vol. II (print anthology)

Love Unexpected series
The Blind Date
The Wrong Man

Johnson Family series
Unforgettable
Perfect
Just Friends (spring 2015)

Bailar series (sweet/clean romance)
Worth Waiting For

Short Stories
Subordinate Position
The Ultimate Merger

Free Stories
www.delaneydiamond.com

ABOUT THE AUTHOR

Delaney Diamond is the USA Today Bestselling Author of sweet, sensual, passionate romance novels. Originally from the U.S. Virgin Islands, she now lives in Atlanta, Georgia. She reads romance novels, mysteries, thrillers, and a fair amount of nonfiction. When she's not busy reading or writing, she's in the kitchen trying out new recipes, dining at one of her favorite restaurants, or traveling to an interesting locale. She speaks fluent conversational French and can get by in Spanish.

Enjoy free reads and the first chapter of all her novels on her website. Join her e-mail mailing list to get sneak peeks, notices of sale prices, and find out about new releases.

http://delaneydiamond.com
https://www.facebook.com/DelaneyDiamond

Made in the USA
Lexington, KY
28 January 2015